HUNTING SEASON

KATE RUDOLPH

CELESTIAL HEART PRESS

WEREWOLF. Bodyguard. Mate.

Owen has one job: keep Stasia from being abducted. Easier said than done when his fiercly independent client tries to fire him the moment they meet. His werewolf senses howl to life and he's certain of one thing: Stasia is his.

She's sick of overbearing men.

When her wealthy father hires a bodyguard, Stasia says no. Not exactly a smart move after someone tried to nab her off the street. But she doesn't need a babysitter. Especially not someone who makes her heart pound and her fantasies run wild.

When Stasia is yanked out of her glittering world and into Owen's she'll need to grapple with an impossible new reality: werewolves exist. And her bodyguard says he's her mate.

 Created with Vellum

Stasia wanted to curse the strength of her cell signal. She hadn't spoken to her father in nearly a year and now he wouldn't stop talking. Where was a dropped call when she needed it?

"Are you there?" he asked for the second time.

She glanced at the nearby entrance to the subway and contemplated running down the stairs. She doubted even that would save her. "I'm here," she confirmed.

"Then speak when you're spoken to."

He couldn't be serious. "You asked me to come to Riley's birthday party." She had to repeat it to make sure she understood. "That would be your wife. Who's ten years younger than me." It didn't exactly grate at this point. His last wife had only been six years older than her. And then there were four others. She'd forgotten most of their names at this point.

"It's not Riley's birthday, it's Emmy's. She's turning three." She heard a sound in the background and wondered what work her father was ignoring for this inane invitation.

"I'm pretty sure Riley's kid is turning four." And she wasn't getting into the name issue. She wanted off this call, not to start a fight.

If only she was still working at the hospital. This would be the perfect moment for an emergency page.

"Emmy is your sister." Armand Selby was a stickler for the facts… when they suited him. And Emmy was Stasia's half-sister. One of her *nine* half-siblings.

But that didn't mean she wanted to drop everything for a toddler's birthday. "I'll have to look at my schedule. I don't know if I'll be in town." She'd known it was a mistake to move back to New York. She was way too close to family obligations that she'd rather ignore.

"You know you can arrange to use the jet if transportation is an issue." He mumbled something, and Stasia was pretty sure she was about to be handed off to an assistant to make plans. The assistants weren't nearly as easy to distract as her father. But at least she didn't feel conflicted about lying to them.

"Transportation isn't the issue." She wasn't going to use the family jet. Or one of the fleet of family cars. Or anything that came from her family's grotesque wealth if she could ignore it. She had an inheritance she already hated to touch, but at least *that* didn't come with strings.

Horns blared down the street and Stasia barely noticed them. Honking horns were just a part of everyday life. But the sound came towards her in a wave, as if warning of some impending doom. She looked down the road, wondering if it was an ambulance or an erratic driver. Another pedestrian bumped into her shoulder and cursed.

Stasia didn't apologize. This was New York.

But she should have kept walking.

She didn't see a car stop, but a hand clamped on her arm and started to pull her towards the road. She dropped her phone as she yelled out and spun around, ready to hit whoever was manhandling her. Her heart jumped into her throat when she saw a scarf around the man's face and dark sunglasses obscuring his eyes. A bit of dark hair peeked out from his navy blue baseball cap, but she could not have described him to save her life.

Neither could any of the thousands of witnesses around them.

They were about to see a woman abducted in broad daylight.

Like hell.

This wasn't Stasia's first rodeo. She reared back, aiming for his throat with the bony point of her elbow. She moved fast enough to jerk out of his grasp, but he flinched back and her strike didn't connect.

"Help! Call the cops!" Stasia called out as the man got a hold of her again. She used her best ER voice, the one she'd learned from the veteran nurses who could make anyone follow an order. And she didn't panic. Panic got a person killed.

The man got a good grip and started pulling her towards a dark car with tinted windows that had appeared at the side of the road. Distantly she wondered if that was who had caused all the cars to honk, but she wasn't about to dwell.

She went limp, dead weight against the man, refusing to be a participant in her abduction. That wasn't something she'd learned in an ER, but rather something one of her bodyguards had instructed her to do as a child.

Stasia looked around, trying to get a better idea of what was happening, who was witnessing it, and who was trying to abduct her. A blonde woman stood wide-eyed with her phone out, getting video of the whole thing.

Video wouldn't do Stasia much good if she got stuffed into the trunk of a car.

"You," she couldn't point, but she made eye contact with the woman, "Call the police! Now!" That was the last thing she could say before her abductor clamped a hand over her mouth.

Stasia tried to bite down on his palm but she didn't have the leverage. She went limp again and winced as her ankle twisted against the hard concrete, but it forced her captor to stumble.

"Let go of her!" a man in a Knicks jersey yelled, shoving his way forward. Stasia managed another glance around and saw they'd drawn another crowd, something not too hard to do on a busy New York street.

So why was someone snatching her here?

She'd worry about that later.

"Let her go!" A young woman with bright purple hair who was wearing a torn jean jacket joined the fray. It only took a minute for the scene to descend into a mob, and Stasia was yanked away from the man. Three or four people surrounded her would-be captor, but he drove his shoulder into the guy wearing the jersey and scuttled back until he was close to the car. A door opened and he dove in as the car drove away.

"Are you okay?" the woman with purple hair asked. She stooped down and held out Stasia's phone. "This yours?"

Stasia's arms were starting to shake and her teeth chattered. Shock. She knew it, but that did nothing to make it go away when she was right in the thick of it. "I'm fine," she managed to say around trembling lips.

"You don't look fine. What did that guy want with you? I've never seen something like that before." The girl shuddered.

Stasia laughed. She knew it wasn't the right response, just another case of neurons misfiring due to trauma. But laughing was better than crying. "I have." And she knew exactly what that guy wanted with her.

Ransom.

Her father's money.

It always came down to that.

For all the privilege that came with wealth, it wasn't always safe to be the daughter of a billionaire.

She looked down at her phone and was surprised to see the screen wasn't cracked. That was truly a miracle. There were a dozen notifications from her father, demanding to know what was going on. Stasia was tempted to leave him hanging. But someone in the crowd around her was bound to post video of the event to social media and the news would be better coming from her. She pulled up her texting app. She didn't think she could manage a conversation with Armand Selby right now.

Attempted kidnapping. Crowd fought attacker off. Bound to be video on social media. Must speak to police shortly. Will contact you for damage control.

There. That covered it. And her fingers were barely shaking anymore. A moment later her phone pinged with the response.

Sending lawyer to you. Remain quiet until you have counsel.

She didn't send anything back. She didn't need to. Another daughter might have chafed at the fact that her father hadn't checked to see if she was alright. Another woman might have been upset that her father instructed her to wait for a lawyer like she was a child. But she'd learned a long time ago that there was no use in getting angry.

The purple haired woman put a hand on Stasia's shoulder and she flinched away.

"Sorry," said the woman. "I'm Vi. I see a couple of

cops coming our way. Do you want me to distract them?"

Stasia took a closer look at Vi. She was young, probably under twenty-five, but there was a hardness to her eyes that only came from being hurt by people you trusted. And here she was trying to help a stranger. She gave off a forbidding enough aura that most of the crowd was keeping back from the two of them. If Stasia was just a bit more jaded, she would think Vi was in on the attack. But her instincts were telling her to trust the girl. "No need. I've got backup incoming." She held up her phone and gave it a little shake.

Two uniformed officers were breaking up the crowd and Stasia braced herself.

"Ma'am," said the first cop. He and his partner looked basically the same and there was no way she was going to remember them. She glanced at the nametags and saw one was named Smith and the other Jones. Lovely. "We had a call come in."

"Someone attempted to kidnap me," she confirmed. Her voice was steadier now and her hands weren't shaking. Good. Cops didn't like crying women. "You're going to want to call your sergeant before the media circus starts."

"Media circus?" Officer Jones was skeptical. "This

is New York, ma'am. Now we need to take your statement."

"My name is Stasia Nichols. My father is Armand Selby, the third richest man in New York. And I won't be saying anything else until my lawyer joins us. Now, shall we speak at the station? Or would you like to wait for the news vans to show up?"

CHAPTER TWO

THE AIR FELT *GREEN*. Owen tipped his head back and howled in joy and abandon into the moon-bright night. The ground was soft under his paws, some of the mud squishing up between his toe pads. He loved it, loved the connection to the earth and to his primal self. Running like this was a freedom he'd never imagined before the change.

Now he couldn't imagine a life without it.

A chorus of howls answered his cry and wind whooshed behind him as one of his team chased after him. Owen glimpsed brown fur, but it was the scent that gave the wolf away. Andre bumped him and nipped at his fur before taking off running. Owen chased. They were safe in these woods. Gibson owned the property and they had miles to run and run and run through dense forest and forgotten paths.

Forgotten to humans, at least.

But in the beautiful chorus of howls, they were missing two. Rowe and Vega were out on a job and were probably running by themselves somewhere that could never live up to these grounds.

Owen let out a little whine at the thought. He wanted his family together. They may not have shared blood, but a dark night had bound them together years ago, and he was determined to build something with the men and women who shifted and ran with him.

Who else could understand how weird it was to be a werewolf?

He'd only been one for two years and he still didn't understand most of it. None of them did. But sometimes the urge to shift overcame them all and they ended up running through the night like the wild beasts that lived inside of them. It wasn't connected to the full moon, that much they had tested. But there weren't exactly guidebooks they could follow.

Andre let out a frustrated bark and Owen shook himself. Those were human thoughts for human time. He let them fall away and surrendered to his wolf. The scents grew more intense and he *knew* a hare was just out of reach, full of juicy blood and the spirit of the run.

He and Andre ran together and it wasn't too long before Hunter, Jackson, and Gibson joined them. One hare would never satisfy five wolves. But hare wasn't the only prey in these woods.

Gibson took the lead. The major had a way of doing that, and they all unconsciously followed. In this form they didn't talk, their communication relegated to looks and chuffs and barks. It didn't take much to get them into formation. They'd done this before.

Hare forgotten, they latched onto the scent of a stag and chased.

Owen's muscles ached but he forgot about it in the euphoria of the hunt. This was what his body was meant to do and he never wanted to stop.

And then it happened. The stag appeared.

The hunt was on.

He no longer paid attention to the feel of the ground beneath his paws or the scent of the trees in the air. His entire being was focused on the stag and the hearty meal they were bound to have. When Owen woke up with two legs he knew he might have a weird taste in his mouth, but he didn't care. He didn't worry about the future in this form.

It was going perfectly. They were a unit born to hunt together.

Andre ran ahead to flush the stag along the right path while the rest of them bounded after it, ready to pounce once it stumbled.

Only something went wrong. The deer was supposed to keep heading along the path. The trees would close in and become too dense for it to go any further. Then it would be theirs.

It didn't.

The stag took a turn toward the east and in a matter of seconds made it to the county road that abutted the property. The wolves had to skid to a stop before they left the tree line. They couldn't risk getting spotted by a regular human. If they were lucky, they might be mistaken for coyotes. But they weren't going to rely on luck.

Owen and the others were disappointed. It was hard not to be when a juicy stag had bounded from their grasp. But the night wasn't ruined. Not by a long shot. They ran and chased and played until exhaustion got the better of them. Some nights, they ended up in a pile of sleeping fur and slept under the stars. Not tonight.

Gibson gave the call and they all headed back towards the cabin.

Before he went in through the basement door, Owen shifted back to human. The others followed shortly behind him. His shift was faster than theirs, but not by much, and thankfully it wasn't too painful for any of them. It felt like stretching his muscles just past the point of comfort and holding it there for several seconds. Not exactly pleasant, but worth the cost.

And once he stood up, naked in the pale moonlight, his senses felt muffled by cotton. He could barely smell anything and the sounds all meshed together. But colors quickly became clearer as his senses adjusted back to human. *That* was the most jarring part of the whole change.

He opened the door and headed inside, picking up his bathrobe that was lying on the floor where he'd left it before the run. Everyone else did the same. They were quiet. They always were when they became human again, as if it took a while to remember how their vocal cords worked and what words went in which order.

Then Owen's stomach grumbled.

"Fuckin' Chip," Erin Jackson groused. She tied her own robe tight and slicked her blonde hair back into a ponytail with a tie that seemed to materialize from nowhere. He didn't know how she got her hair slicked so perfectly and he wasn't about to ask.

Jackson had a way of frowning that made him sure he was about to get hit.

"Chip's hungry, major," Andre Gordon told Gibson, as if the major couldn't hear Owen's stomach.

Owen kept quiet and clamped a hand over his stomach as if that would do something to quiet it down. Then his stomach growled again and he couldn't hold in his laugh. "What can I say? I wanted venison!"

Gibson rolled his eyes. "Too fucking chipper is right. Hunter, go up and order a few pizzas. The usual place should still be open." It was getting close to midnight, but they were on the edge of a college town and plenty of places were open until the wee hours.

Willa Hunter had managed to pull actual clothes on while the others were teasing him. She gave the major a nod before hurrying up the stairs without a word. Owen tried to wave, but she was already out of sight. Oh well. At least she knew the pizza order.

Owen went to find his clothes before anyone else could rib him for his grumbling tummy. He checked his phone and wasn't surprised to see no new messages. He'd called his mother earlier in the day so she had no reason to call, and if something had gone wrong with Vega or Rowe they would have called Gibson or Gordon. Owen wasn't anyone's first call.

The cabin was big enough that he and the others weren't stepping all over each other to store their clothes or move around. Since it was already past midnight, they'd probably be staying the night. It was more than an hour's drive back into the city, and it wouldn't be the first night they'd all slept over. Owen suspected that Gibson came from money, but he'd never asked. He was pretty sure the major could still majorly fuck with his life even though they'd all been retired from the army for two years. He wasn't about to test the man.

The cabin had two large bedrooms in the basement and another two upstairs. The major took the master; no one questioned it. Hunter and Jackson both managed to snag their own rooms, which left Owen and Andre to share. He didn't mind. It wasn't like Andre snored.

Owen considered taking a quick shower, but his skin felt all fresh and new from the shift so there was no need. Some of the tiredness from running around on all fours all night was starting to catch up to him, and he wanted to crawl into his bed, but Gibson would want a check in.

And Owen wanted pizza.

He went upstairs and found everyone dressed

and sitting around the large kitchen island, devouring the first of four pepperoni and mushroom pizzas. Owen cracked into the next pizza and took four pieces. That was another thing about being a werewolf. They had to eat *all the time.* Their bodies devoured calories like it was going out of style. And Owen ate the first slices so fast that he barely tasted them.

"Any update on the Bradley job?" Jackson asked. She took dainty bites of her pizza and dabbed at her lips with a napkin to wipe away the grease after every bite.

Gibson nodded to the cell phone sitting beside his plate. "Rowe texted. Job's wrapping up. They'll be home in a couple of days."

Some of the tension—tension Owen hadn't quite realized he was feeling—leeched out of the unit. It was good to know they'd all be together again. "Any issues?" he asked, mouth full of pizza.

Gibson glared at him and Owen grinned wider. "All was well. The ex did not show up to the wedding and the happy couple are on their way to Aruba."

The news wasn't exactly momentous and no one cheered. "Anything more interesting that babysitting a couple of brides come up?" asked Andre. He was slouched in the corner and somehow managed to be half cloaked in shadow despite the brightly lit kitchen. There was just a hint of menace in his voice and Owen wanted to roll his eyes. The guy was all drama and needed to learn to chill. They'd just gone for a run. They had pizza. What was there to complain about?

Two years before, after they'd been unceremoniously dumped out of the army in an attempt to keep what had happened to them hush hush, Gibson had gathered them all together with an idea: protection. They could provide it to those in need all while figuring out what it meant to be impossible creatures in an ordinary world. Their bodyguarding outfit had gotten off the ground eighteen months ago, but they were still making a name for themselves. That involved taking small jobs and networking. Owen didn't mind it. He was pretty sure that Andre would rather jump off a building than make nice with potential clients.

"You'll be the first to know," Gibson promised, voice dripping with sarcasm.

Andre glared from his dark corner.

Just as Gibson was ready to stuff another piece of pizza in his mouth, his phone rang. He looked at the screen for a moment, eyes narrowed, then put the pizza down, picked up the phone, and walked outside.

He shot Andre a look and then glanced at Jackson and Hunter, then they all looked out at Gibson. He was standing on the balcony and had closed the sliding glass door. Owen wished being a werewolf had given him super hearing. His research—if watching *Teen Wolf* counted as research—had suggested he should be able to do a lot more than he could. He was a bit stronger, a bit faster, his senses were a bit more acute, but nothing inhuman. Nothing that would allow any of them to actually hear what the major was saying.

"He's being secretive," Hunter muttered.

Owen had to bite his lip from saying something. Hunter wouldn't even tell them her birthday or hometown. "The major's allowed to have a private call."

"No, that was weird," Jackson agreed. She glanced at each of their plates as if counting the number of pieces they'd had and then reached for the next pizza box.

The four of them stared at Gibson through the glass as they chomped on their pizza. Only once he hung up the phone did they swing around to pretend they hadn't been shamelessly snooping.

"You're all very subtle," Gibson said once he slid the door shut. "Myers, with me." He nodded down the hallway towards his bedroom.

Owen had the strangest sense of being called to the principal's office. He had to remind himself he wasn't in school or the army anymore and no one could hurt him.

Yeah, right. The major could make his life hell if he wanted. Owen tried to think if he'd done anything wrong in the past week or so, but nothing came to mind. And then he reminded himself that he was thirty-two goddamn years old and he didn't need to be afraid of Gibson.

He entered Gibson's bedroom and closed the door behind him. They were far enough away from the others not to be overheard as long as they spoke quietly, and this bedroom doubled as Gibson's office when he was at the cabin, so it wasn't strange to have a discussion here.

"What's up?" Owen asked. He leaned back against the door and crossed his arms loosely.

Gibson sat at the small desk he had set up and opened the lid to his laptop. "That was a friend of mine from college. His sister might be in trouble and he wants a guard on her for the next week while his family takes care of it."

"Takes care of it? Is he the mob?" They didn't have a strict moral code about who they would work for, but Owen figured there had to be a line *somewhere.*

Gibson huffed out a little laugh. "Worse. Money. Big money. You ever hear of the Selbys?"

"Can't say that I have." Owen knew his famous rich people, but not the sneaky ones who stayed out of the limelight.

"The Selby Group has its fingers in every pie. Old money. The daughter isn't involved, but this is the second attempted kidnapping of her in three years."

"Kidnapping? That's a bit more than trouble." Owen had expected to hear about another babysitting gig. Heiresses were needy like that.

"AR sounds sure the private family security could handle it, but he wanted an outsider to watch his sister. Apparently she's not a fan of family security and he thought this would work better. I'm sending you."

"Just me?" Owen didn't mind flying solo, but that wasn't how missions worked. He couldn't cover 24/7, enhanced werewolf senses or not. He had to sleep sometime.

"To begin with, yes. He wants to convince her to accept a team, but he's going to ease her into it. There will be support monitoring from a distance, but you'll be her only point of contact."

"Our support or their support?" Owen didn't like the idea of going in alone, and he really didn't like the idea of strange backup. But he went where the major ordered.

"Theirs." Gibson didn't sound too happy about it either.

Owen couldn't see the point in arguing; Gibson wanted him for the job so he would do it. "When do I start?"

Gibson turned back to his computer and typed a few things. A moment later, Owen's phone chimed. "Show up bright and early tomorrow. I've sent you the details."

"Guess I'm heading back to the city tonight." He stood. "Anything else?"

Gibson leveled a glare at him. "Don't fuck this up."

"Yes, sir."

CHAPTER THREE

OWEN YAWNED and stretched his neck from side to side, satisfied to hear the pops and cracks of muscle and bone releasing. Or whatever caused a neck to crack. He wasn't sure. It sounded awful but felt amazing. He took a sip of his gigantic iced coffee and imagined he could feel the caffeine starting to flow through his system. He'd asked for three extra shots of espresso and a buttload of sugar and cream to offset the bitterness.

The barista hadn't batted an eye. He was sure she'd seen much worse.

He didn't know if it was werewolf metabolism or years of resistance, but it took a *lot* of coffee to wake him up, especially after a run. And the drive to the city in the middle of the night had been annoying. But he was glad he hadn't waited. He could hear the horns of the cars weaving through the streets of Manhattan and was grateful he'd only had to drive across town and not across the state.

Normally he wouldn't be using a car. This was New York. Who had a car? But on a job it was a necessity. It was much easier to keep someone safe in a car as opposed to on the subway. And Gibson had provided everyone in the company with specially outfitted cars. They weren't *technically* armored, but he'd seen tanks that could take less damage. The car was stored in a parking garage a block away. Unfortunately, the client's building didn't have a secure parking garage and there was no extra space in their small lot for him to park. As far as challenges went, he could deal with it.

The building was nicer than he expected, but maybe it shouldn't have been. No ER doctor could have afforded the place. It had to cost millions. But his charge, Stasia Nichols, was no normal doctor. The pre-war building was only a few blocks away from the hospital she'd formerly worked at, which would have been convenient. The doorman on the building offered an extra piece of security, and that meant Dr. Nichols was smart enough to know there might be a target on her head.

Or she just liked it when someone in a uniform opened a door for her.

Owen gave the man a smile as he was let in. Selby Group security had arranged everything except giving him a key to Stasia's unit.

He eyed the elevator before opting for the stairs. The elevator looked original to the building—built in 1909—and Owen didn't want to take his chances. Of course, people rich enough to afford digs in this building would insist that the machine functioned. But he didn't like it and he was already running a little late.

Stasia lived in one of the two units on the fifth and sixth floor. The entrance to her unit was on the fifth floor and he wasn't winded by the time he climbed all those steps: army training and werewolf stamina for the win.

He took a bracing sip of his coffee. He didn't know how this was going to go, and he usually had a partner right beside him to smooth over any issues that came up. Owen was good at his job, great, actually, but he could ruffle feathers. Never on purpose, but not everyone reacted well to his default level of optimism.

He mentally went over the file he'd been given. All the data was saved on his phone, but he didn't need to bring it up. There wasn't much to know. Stasia was a pretty princess who'd traveled the world on daddy's money after becoming a doctor. After cutting her international vacation short, she'd set up shop in New York, working in the ER department of a nearby hospital, though she'd recently been fired. No reason in the file, but Owen could guess that spoiled princesses weren't exactly cut out for the ER.

She'd been raised with bodyguards all around her. Her father was one of the richest men in the city, she knew the drill. The job would be easy. With her father's security team tackling most of the tough stuff—investigating who'd tried to attack her and providing backup surveillance—Owen's job was mostly to sit around and look pretty. Or threatening. He could be a good guard dog. And at the end of the week, the job would be over, he'd have a paycheck, Gibson would have paid off a favor, and hopefully there would be more interesting jobs coming his way.

Hopefully.

But Owen couldn't slack just because he expected a boring job. That was the surest way to get his charge and himself killed.

He took another sip of coffee for good measure and knocked on the door and waited.

And waited.

And waited.

Then he knocked again. Didn't the princess know he was coming?

Maybe he needed to be kinder; after all, she had

almost been kidnapped right off the street yesterday. That would make him wary of opening the door too.

But he finally heard footsteps and a moment later the door opened.

Owen forgot how to breathe.

His file had a picture of Stasia Nichols, but it didn't do her justice. Her big gray eyes reminded him of the moon and he couldn't look away. She had black hair hanging down and framing her pale face and full lips that he needed to kiss. She was shorter than he expected, but she exuded a presence that made her seem taller than him, even with only the single look they shared.

He wanted to reach out and put his hands on the curve of her hips and run them all over her body. He'd never been overtaken by such instant lust before and he could feel his wolf rustling under his skin, restless and wanting to preen for their…

Their what?

Their?

He didn't normally think of his wolf as something separate from himself. Sometimes he was a man, sometimes he was a wolf, but he was always Owen, no matter how much fur he had. But right now he could feel the presence of something… different. Something primal.

His cock twitched and Owen clenched his jaw.

This was not the time. He'd guarded plenty of attractive charges before and had always been able to keep it professional. This was no different.

But none of them were Stasia.

Her scent tickled his nose and there went his wolf again. He could practically feel his tail wagging in excitement. But now was not the time for tail wagging from *either* of his tails.

"Did you move in across the hall?" she asked. Her expression was severe, like a smile would physically pain her, but somehow it charmed Owen. He knew that when he got her to smile it would be because he earned it.

He didn't understand what she meant at first and looked over his shoulder to the other door. That unit must have been empty. He'd have to update the file to make sure everyone knew. It probably should have been in the file already.

"Well?" she asked when he waited too long to answer.

Owen snapped back to her. "I'm here for your body." The words were all English, but he could have smacked himself for the way they came out.

"*Excuse* me?" Stasia's dark eyebrows shot up and she looked ready to slap him.

"No, no!" Owen waved his hands, trying to correct himself. "To guard your body. I'm your bodyguard. Owen Myers." He never got tongue-tied. He might never be the smartest in the room, but he always knew what to say. Except, apparently, when his wolf and his cock and his brain all had other ideas.

"Oh." Stasia's eyes flicked up and down, and when she met his eyes again he knew he'd been judged. And he'd failed. "No."

"What?"

"No." She said it slow, elongating the word as if she thought he was too stupid to understand.

Then again, this was not his best first impression. Maybe he should have added a fourth shot of espresso. "I'm sorry for any misunderstanding. The Selby Group hired my firm to watch over you while they investigate the attempted kidnapping. We just want to keep you safe."

Her dark eyes narrowed and she pursed her lips. "Tell my father I'm safe enough as it is."

And before he had a chance to say anything else, she slammed the door in his face.

CHAPTER FOUR

Stasia kept her hand on the door as if that would keep the stupid, meddling, *attractive* bodyguard from busting through.

She should have known he was coming. Her father and her brother had let this whole situation drop way too easily last night. After a few hours at the police station where she'd given a report and done her best to guide the detectives toward an explanation for what had happened, she'd been able to go home and pretend that everything was going to be okay. She'd even allowed her father to leave a security detail outside of her building overnight.

Just in case something went wrong.

That had been a mistake. She should have known her father wouldn't stop there.

Owen Myers didn't look like any of the guards that her father normally hired. He wasn't even wearing a suit. And the smile he flashed her—white teeth, laugh lines, kissable lips, and warm, tanned skin—was enough to make her stomach flutter.

Not that she would ever let him know that.

He was too hot for his own good and no doubt he knew it. He was too hot for *her* own good too. Just looking at him made her think of sultry nights and humid air.

She couldn't remember ever having inappropriate feelings for a bodyguard before, and she wasn't about to start now. She didn't need a bodyguard. Sure, maybe she had almost been snatched off the street in broad daylight. That wasn't ideal. But that was her father's bullshit. It had *nothing* to do with her, and she wasn't about to start getting involved in whatever nonsense the Selby Group was cooking up.

She didn't work for her father's company.

She didn't live in his house.

She didn't have to deal with his edicts anymore.

A hollow knock echoed right beside her ear. "Ms. Nichols, please let me in." All that was bodyguard voice. Cold and commanding, the kind that was supposed to make her want to jump to attention. Stasia hated that a part of her wanted to shiver and obey.

But it was only a small part, and she didn't give in that easy. "It's *doctor*." She'd worked long and hard for that degree and she wasn't about to let anybody forget about it.

"*Dr.* Nichols," he corrected. "Please let me in."

"No." This was ridiculous. She was yelling at a bodyguard through her own closed door like she needed to bargain to make him go away. He wasn't getting into the room without forcing his way in, and if he tried he would be fired before he could get past the first lock.

Her father had some nerve. She'd allowed the detail to follow her because it seemed logical. But she did not need a bulldog watching her every step. Who did this guy think he was?

And what kind of bodyguard looked like he had walked right off a runway somewhere?

He was almost a full head taller than her, definitely a couple inches over six feet. He had short dark hair and soulful brown eyes lined with just enough laugh lines to make him look sweet and gentle… and oh so sexy. He had the kind of even tan that only came naturally, and even though he was covered from head to toe, she could tell there were muscles rippling just below the surface. He wasn't the kind of guy she normally found herself attracted to.

Mostly because he was the kind of guy that only existed in pornographic fantasies.

There were plenty of hot doctors around, and hot lawyers, and hot stockbrokers, and hot baristas. But none of them held a candle to this Owen guy.

It was too bad she had to ruin his life. Okay, that was probably a *bit* of an exaggeration. She just wanted to get him fired, she didn't care about the rest of his life.

She wasn't going to let him come in to boss her around and babysit her.

She didn't need it.

She didn't want it.

She wasn't going to have it.

He knocked on the door again, but he didn't say anything this time. Stasia stared at the white wood for a long moment before pushing off and heading deeper into her condo. Let him stew. She didn't owe him anything. Eventually he would realize that she wasn't listening.

And luckily she didn't have a neighbor, so even if he decided to wait outside her front door all day no one would be there to question his presence. She didn't *really* care if the neighbors started to gossip, but she had decades of media training that made her shy away from the spotlight unless she was using it to her advantage.

No one could break into her apartment to kidnap her if he was standing right outside the door.

She hated that she even thought it. She hated that a small part of her wanted to let him inside to take care of all of her problems and guard her until whatever problem her father had caused in her life was fixed by her father's money.

But she'd learned a long time ago that letting her father dictate any aspect of her life led to him dictating *every* aspect.

It started small, logical. Someone tried to kidnap her so he offered personal protection. If they couldn't catch the guy, he would say she should move into his penthouse since it was more secure than her building. Was that true? Sure. But she'd sacrifice a lot of personal security to stay out from under her father's thumb.

She didn't have a job at the hospital anymore, and he had plenty of contacts who would be happy to hire her. And just like that, she would be wrapped up in a web of favors and responsibilities that she could never escape.

She knew who her father was. He didn't love like a normal person. Some thought he was completely incapable of the emotion, but she knew it was more complex than that. To him, love was transactional. None of his wives had ever lived up to the concept, and she and her nine siblings fell in and out of favor depending on his moods and their usefulness. Well, maybe the baby got a pass. For now.

In another life, he would have been a king or a lord, dictating his will and whims out on the world. He didn't have a title, but he still used his wealth in the exact same way.

She was free of him now, more or less. And she couldn't let this be another setback. It had taken nearly two years to climb her way out of the last setback that put her in her father's clutches. She didn't want to start all over again.

Even if starting over was exactly what she was doing right now. But at least it had nothing to do with her father.

She picked her phone up from the kitchen counter and tried her father's number. She wasn't surprised when he didn't pick up and she was immediately forwarded to his assistant's answering service. She hung up before leaving a message. If he wanted to talk he would have picked up.

Then she tried AR. If her father couldn't be reached, her oldest brother was almost as good. He was their father's right-hand man and heir. He did the family dirty work.

But AR didn't answer either.

Stasia cursed and set the phone back down. She hated the games her family played. No doubt her father and AR were busy. They would be able to give her a dozen convenient and logical reasons why they couldn't answer her calls.

But in reality, they weren't answering because they thought if they ignored her for long enough she would give up and accept that Owen was going to be her shadow until they decided she was safe.

Safe.

She didn't think she could ever truly be safe as long as she was the daughter of Armand Selby. And short of time travel, there wasn't a way to untie that knot.

Owen knocked on the door again, an unwelcome reminder of all of the control that her father tried to wield over her.

She ignored him and instead consulted the calendar app on her phone to see what she had to do today. She'd been trying to keep herself busy in the couple weeks since she had left her previous job and she was happy to see that she had a volunteer shift coming up.

She eyed the window in her sitting room that looked out over Gramercy Park. If her apartment was just a few stories lower, she would have been happy to sneak out and lose the guard dog. But she had stopped playing games with security details when she was a teenager. She was a thirty-four-year-old adult woman now.

If she didn't want to be followed, she would just have to lose him the old-fashioned way.

CHAPTER FIVE

Owen pressed his fingers against the door. Solid. Mahogany? Maybe. Definitely fancy and hard. Nothing he could bust down. Not that he would. That would give exactly the opposite impression that he wanted to give to Stasia.

He could barely hear her walking around inside the condo. The sound of her footsteps was mostly drowned out by his own beating heart, but at least he knew she was safe and sound where she was supposed to be. He'd have to figure out another way inside.

It wasn't like he was going to hold her prisoner. Though his mind did briefly flash on a pair of fuzzy handcuffs he'd once been chained to a bed with. Would she be into that?

Definitely not something he would ask. He wasn't *that* stupid.

If he couldn't get inside the condo and he couldn't get her to agree to protection, his presence was useless. But Owen didn't panic. Sometimes clients got cold feet when their guards showed up. It made the whole thing more real. He'd probably be freaked out too.

Though he doubted there were many baddies out there who could take down a freaking werewolf.

The princess wasn't who he'd expected. He wasn't easy to stare down and ignore, and she'd done it like it was nothing. Definitely not some precious flower.

He wanted to test her boundaries. Wanted to see if he could make that sour face of hers crack a smile. And he wanted to taste her lips more than he wanted his next breath. The attraction wasn't fading, even as the minutes passed and she kept ignoring him.

His wolf didn't like that.

He and his wolf needed to have a talk. He couldn't deal with a split personality in the middle of a job.

He pulled out his phone and called Gibson. It was embarrassing to have the door slammed in his face, but he still needed to report it to his boss.

Gibson answered on the first ring. "You all set?" Owen could hear road noise in the background of the call and assumed the boss was coming back to the city.

"Negative. Client wouldn't let me in." He traced his finger up and down a patch of the door as if that would magically open it.

The major didn't like that. "What?"

Owen let out a frustrated breath. "Seems like a family squabble. I'm working on it."

"Do you need me to call the brother?"

Owen considered it, but dismissed it. "Give me a bit more time. I'll let you know." He didn't want to call in reinforcements just yet. Maybe he could get the princess to deal with him.

"Affirmative." Gibson hung up without bothering with any pleasantries. He had more jobs to manage and wouldn't bother Owen until the next report.

He was about to put his phone in his pocket when it vibrated with an incoming call. "This is Myers."

"Peters with Selby Security." He didn't know the man, but the company was obvious.

"You're on the surveillance team?" What was wrong? Hostile in the area? Had they detained the attempted kidnappers? Owen forced himself not to hound the man for answers; clearly he was calling for a reason.

"Yes. Confirming Ms. Selby's exit."

"It's doctor." The correction came automatically

and then his brain caught up. "Wait. What? What exit?"

"We have eyes on her out the back exit. Where are you?" asked Peters.

Not good. Not good. Not good.

It was a rookie move to let the client slip out the back like a teenager breaking curfew, and he hoped it didn't get her killed. "Fuck. Hold. I'm coming."

"Shall we detain?" Peters was all professionalism, which was good because Owen was ready to beat himself bloody for his stupidity.

"No. Keep eyes on her." He didn't want her hating him or the security detail even more. There was time to fix this.

If he hurried.

He sprinted down the stairs and towards the back of the building. Of course, Stasia was already gone. She had a few minutes on him, but that wouldn't be a problem. No doubt Mr. Peters had eyes on her, but Owen wanted to find her himself.

His wolfish instincts hummed.

Going out the back was clever, if juvenile. And he hadn't expected it. Dr. Nichols kept messing with his expectations and he'd need to reassess.

Her street wasn't crowded, but it was still New York. Scents and people swirled all around him, and Owen had to concentrate to figure out where to go.

He didn't see her at first and he had no idea where she was going. But it was only a matter of time.

There!

She was standing at a stoplight and making no attempt to hide her identity. She had to know the surveillance team could see her, and he hoped that was on purpose. She didn't want *him*, that didn't make her suicidal.

He hung back but didn't care about staying out of sight. She'd see him if she looked over her shoulder, but there wasn't anything he could do about that short of shifting into his other form, and *that* would certainly attract more attention than it was worth.

She ducked into a coffee shop, giving Owen the opportunity to throw his own watery coffee into a nearby trashcan. He didn't follow her inside. At this point he was curious to see what she was going to do. There were plenty of eyes on her, and he had no reason to believe that the people targeting her would physically harm her. He was going to let this play out.

She had to know he was following her. She sipped her coffee as they walked a few more blocks, then dumped it in a garbage can.

Was this whole thing a simple coffee run?

No.

She took the stairs down into the subway and

Owen followed, closing some of the distance between them. He didn't want her getting on a train without him.

What the fuck was she thinking? No way would the surveillance team be able to keep up.

He hoped they were tracking her phone.

The train was already there and not too crowded. There must have been a lull in the commute, or they were lucky. Stasia took a seat.

Owen sat next to her.

"Looks like you're not as much of an idiot as you look," she said as she situated her purse on her lap.

"Hey!" That stung a bit. Owen wasn't dumb. He just didn't think things through all the time.

Stasia glared at him.

That glare did things and Owen needed to look away, or he definitely wouldn't be thinking things through. "We need to work together."

"You seem to be doing just fine." She was determined to make him beg.

But this was Owen's job and he wasn't playing. "I don't think you're taking this seriously. You were almost kidnapped."

Her eyes flicked to him and then away, unimpressed. "They failed. My father is looking into it. What more can I do?"

"Take a cab?" That had to be obvious. There were

only a few passengers in this car with them, but there could have been a hundred, any one of whom could have meant Stasia harm.

She snorted. "And let my would be kidnappers car jack me? No, thanks."

He wasn't sure the subway was safer than a cab, but at least she'd considered it. Owen would count that as a win, though he wasn't sure what game they were playing or how it was scored.

"Where are we headed now?" He was at her side. They could start over. No reason to call this morning a loss just yet.

But Stasia wasn't about to play along. "I don't know where *you're* going."

"I'm your shadow."

She shifted in her seat to face him, arms crossed and face hard. "I'm not stupid. I'll be vigilant. I neither need nor want you. So go back to my father and tell him that."

"That's not how this works."

"That's *exactly* how this works."

The train screeched to a halt and Stasia jumped up from her seat. Owen had to scramble to follow, and it seemed like their time for conversation was over. He didn't recognize the neighborhood they were in, but it was a world away from the glittering richness of Gramercy Park.

Definitely not the kind of place a spoiled rich girl would hang out.

Unless she was getting drugs.

He hoped she wasn't getting drugs.

She wasn't. Not unless St. Agnes Charity Health Clinic was some kind of front. She got to the front door and stopped quickly enough that Owen almost bumped into her.

"Patients have a right to privacy. I can't stop you from sitting in the waiting area, I suppose. But you step one foot out of line and I'm calling the cops."

She opened the door and let it fall closed right in his face.

Again.

Owen needed to stop letting her do that.

CHAPTER SIX

Stasia punched the keys of the computer harder than necessary as she looked up the chart for her next patient. The volunteer clinic couldn't schedule her for enough hours due to their own internal rules so she wanted to make every minute count.

What she *didn't* want to be thinking about was the sexy, frustrating bodyguard who was probably sitting in the waiting room right now.

"Rough night?" Luna Sparks was a nurse at the clinic and Stasia's friend. Her stark black hair and tattoos didn't really fit in with the vibe of the Catholic charity clinic, but she was an amazing nurse and no one wanted to make her upset.

Stasia wasn't sure how they'd become friends. She wasn't good at talking to people, but Luna had slipped through her defenses like it was nothing.

Even so, she didn't want to bring her stupid, rich girl bullshit into the clinic. She wanted to pretend she was normal, and that meant ignoring the attempted kidnapping and definitely ignoring Owen.

"Something like that." Stasia kept scanning the file, as if that would be enough to make Luna go away.

She smiled, showing big, bright white teeth rimmed by dark red lips. "Who's that guy you walked in with? He's yummy."

"And what would your girlfriend say about that?" Stasia barely glanced up as she shot off the rejoinder. This was proof Luna was her friend. She knew next to nothing about the other people who worked at the clinic. But she knew Luna's girlfriend's name, Gerry, that she was a Gemini with a Cancer rising sign, whatever that meant, and that Luna and Gerry were co-parenting a bearded dragon named Newt.

Luna just laughed. "He's *yummy*. We both have eyes. Do I need to give you the pansexuality lecture again?"

"Please don't." There had been a PowerPoint involved. Stasia now understood more about Luna's sexual orientation than she did about her own, and she really didn't want to sit through another talk.

"So?" Luna pressed.

"Just ignore him and hope he goes away." That

was what Stasia planned to do. She knew it was childish to leave her house like she had, but she wanted to scream at the way Owen had been sprung on her. She hadn't agreed, and she wasn't going to just put up with her family's high handedness.

"Did a stray follow you home?" Luna peered around a corner as if that would allow her to look through the plexiglass window that looked out into the waiting area. It wouldn't, the angle was all wrong, but Stasia wasn't about to stop her.

"Something like that." Thankfully, Stasia was done looking at the file and could escape the conversation to go see her patient and discuss the weird sores he was getting on his feet.

One patient led to the next, and by the end of her four hour shift, Stasia was starting to feel like she could use a break. She'd happily keep checking on people all day, but she was only scheduled for four hours anyway.

She washed her hands and combed her fingers through her hair to try and make it look a little tamer before retying it in a low bun. "Is he still out there?" she asked Luna, who was entering her own information into the computer.

"Like I have time to check," she said with a nod at the computer, and Stasia was sympathetic. Everything needed to be logged, and it could take up way more time than expected. "There's something I wanted to mention."

"Yeah?" Luna sounded serious and that had Stasia's attention.

The nurse looked around surreptitiously like she was planning something, and Stasia's heart rate skyrocketed as she feared her friend was in on the kidnapping plot. Then she spoke, and Stasia wanted to smack herself for thinking that everything was about herself. "I'm applying for a new position."

"Oh. That's... great." But her tone belied her words. Stasia was great under pressure, but not always great with change. It was why her entire life was a bit stalled at the moment. And she liked Luna. She didn't want to break in a whole new nurse, or lose a friend.

Luna spun around on the stool to better face Stasia. "I'm sorry to abandon you, but it's a great opportunity."

"You're not abandoning me." Jobs changed, this was fine. Really. Stasia would get over it.

But Luna still wasn't done talking. "I just know your schedule is sporadic. I didn't want to disappear on you."

Right. That would have been much worse. Luna was her friend, and Stasia didn't know if it would last beyond this job, but at least Luna was warning her. "Thanks for letting me know. And good luck."

Luna had to go help a patient, and Stasia couldn't stick around. She had another meeting to go to, though this one wasn't on any schedule.

As she stepped outside, she didn't see Owen or her security detail, but she was sure they were following. Her father didn't hire imbeciles. She headed back down to the subway and got on a train towards Midtown.

Owen magically appeared next to her, and Stasia hated that she was a little relieved. That half a second where she'd thought Luna was about to betray her had been a shock, and the trauma of yesterday was still a little too close.

"Where are we going now?" Owen asked with a smile, his dark hair ruffled and dangerously sexy.

She hated it. How was this guy so upbeat? And hot? She had treated him like crap, ignored him for hours, and now he was all smiles. What was wrong with him?

"I guess you'll find out."

They didn't speak any more. Stasia had been talking to patients for hours and it was tiring. She didn't need to spar with the guy she was about to get rid of.

Their stop came up fast and Owen followed her off the train without a word. Men and women in suits crowded the Midtown sidewalks and Stasia kept a wary eye out, certain one of these people meant her harm.

No one accosted them and they made it safely to the Selby Building, its signature door surrounded by twisting crimson sculpted lines almost as familiar as home after all these years.

She already had her badge ready and waved it across the sensor to get into the elevator to go to the executive floor. Her father's office was the biggest, of course, with windows that wrapped around the corner and allowed him to look out over all of Manhattan.

When she was little, she used to think looking out of these windows let her see the entire world.

Her father wasn't sitting behind his desk, and the surface of the desk was completely empty, a sign that he wasn't coming back for the day.

One of his assistants, Melody, if Stasia recalled the name correctly, came in. She wore a lavender pant suit and had her blonde hair held back in a tight bun. "He flew out for a meeting this morning. Is there something I can help you with, Dr. Nichols?"

Stasia liked Melody. She hoped her father didn't end up marrying her when he got bored with Riley. "My brother?" she asked. AR was a decent substitute.

"I'll get him." Melody hurried out of the office.

Owen stood quietly beside her as they waited, swaying a little as if he couldn't quite manage to keep still. She wanted to reach a hand out to stop him from moving, but she feared a part of that was just because she wanted an excuse to touch him.

No. She wasn't doing that.

Thankfully, AR walked in before Stasia's baser instincts could take over. At forty-four, AR was ten years older than her and the heir apparent to their father's empire. He was the oldest, the only child from her father's first marriage, and the man she and her siblings turned to when they couldn't get ahold of Armand Selby.

It didn't mean they were close. Stasia tried to think of the last time she'd seen her brother. Thanksgiving? Christmas? No, he'd skipped the holidays because of a work event. No matter what, it had been months.

AR took a seat behind their father's desk like he owned it and placed a leather bound folio in front of him. He gestured for her and Owen to take their seats, but Stasia remained standing. Owen followed her lead.

Interesting.

"I was pulled off an important call for this." AR blew out a breath in frustration.

"I'm sure." Every call was important when billions were on the line. But she could make this easy enough. "Fire him and you can get right back to exploiting poverty-stricken nations."

Owen's head snapped her way, mouth dropping open. "Really?"

"Really?" Her brother was more droll.

Stasia wanted to pace, but she focused all that energy internally and spoke. "I agreed to the detail while you looked into the issue. Surveillance at a distance. Not a full time babysitter."

"I'm not—"

"Talking right now." She shot Owen a glare as she spoke, just to make sure he understood. Owen might have been present, but this wasn't his conversation.

AR leaned back in their father's chair and crossed his arms. "I want you safe."

She believed it—she and AR weren't close, but they were still family. That didn't mean he got to make decisions for her, though. "And your people can't keep me safe enough?"

"Stas…"

"Answer my question." Selby Group employed utterly competent people and Stasia had already made a big concession to allow them to watch her.

But AR had clearly expected this. He opened up the folio on the desk to reveal a tablet. He swiped at the screen to wake it up and then scrolled to find what he was looking for before swiveling it around for her to take a look.

Stasia approached the desk and looked, but she wasn't sure what she was seeing.

"Security found evidence of surveillance in an empty condo across the street from yours," he told her as he scrolled to the next image, which showed an empty apartment. "When we scanned your phone they found spyware. They removed it. This wasn't random and it could happen again. Your best shot at safety is to let..." he looked at Owen as he trailed off and then continued, "Gibson's guy protect you."

Stasia felt strangely offended that AR hadn't bothered to learn Owen's name. If he wanted to know something, he knew it. "His name is Owen. Who the fuck is Gibson?"

Owen spoke up. "My boss."

"A friend," AR added. "I knew you wouldn't trust one of my men so close to you. *Owen* doesn't report to me—not your comings and goings, not your job, nothing but direct threats to your safety. I know you, Stas, give me a bit of credit."

She really didn't want to. But AR had thought this through. It wasn't like she thought this was some big conspiracy between AR and Owen to watch her every move. She appreciated that her brother had thought about her feelings.

She pulled the tablet closer and scrolled through the pictures. There were the telltale white bricks of her building. And there was Gramercy Park. It was where she lived her life.

A shiver threatened to overtake her and her fingers started to shake. Owen took half a step closer to her, as if he sensed her unease. Strangely, that made her feel a little better.

"You said this will be taken care of in a week?" Her voice didn't shake. She didn't sound scared. Good.

"I hope so. My investigators are good. If it drags on for more than a week, we reassess."

She didn't like the thought of the investigation going longer, but it had to be acknowledged. "Is this worse than Bermeja?" She'd hoped *that* would be the worst attack of her life, and since she'd had to overhaul her entire career afterwards, she didn't want to experience it again.

A dark look crossed AR's face. "They put hands on you."

"I don't want to uproot my life again." She'd had a path, a mission. All that was gone now.

"I'm going to make sure that doesn't happen. We like you here in New York." He said it with enough conviction that she almost believed him. Then his tone shifted to something falsely joyous. "You're coming to the birthday party, right?"

"I don't get to claim attempted kidnapping to get out of that? I've seen the kid once!" What was it with the kid's birthday party? What toddler wanted full grown, childless adults hanging out around her?

Her brother laughed, showing no mercy. "She's our sister. And you have a bodyguard."

"Half-sister." She turned to Owen with a sour look. "You're fired."

That declaration startled a laugh out of her bodyguard.

"It won't be that bad," AR tried to reassure her.

Stasia had been down this road before. "We'll see…" Then her mind snagged on a worry that had been percolating for awhile. "Are they after me because of anything the company is doing? Should I know anything?"

"We won't let you get hurt," he promised.

That wasn't an answer, and as she and Owen left, she couldn't help but wonder what her brother and the Selby Group were hiding.

CHAPTER SEVEN

Stasia had a library. Of course she did. Wasn't that a requirement of rich people in these kind of places? The cherry paneling gave the entire room an old world feel that was at odds with what Owen had observed of the doctor. And it made the room dark, despite the sunshine streaming in through the windows. Three lamps were shining bright to combat the darkness, and there were still pockets of shadow around the room.

Judging by the desk, the library doubled as Stasia's office, but the two large couches made it a decent place to have a meeting with the security detail. This was the first time Owen was officially meeting anyone other than Peters, and he wanted to make sure they were just who Stasia needed to keep her safe.

Peters was backed up by Doug Griffin, Rene Beaufort, Russ Hill, Jessie Morgan, and Cathy Rivera. The six person team was working in three shifts with hours overlapping so four people would be watching Stasia during the core hours of eight AM to eight PM. Stasia wasn't the type to go out much on weeknights, apparently, so night coverage was less than day.

From the way the surveillance team sat, Owen was willing to guess that half of them were ex-military: Beaufort, Morgan, and Rivera. He wasn't sure about the others. His attention kept snagging on Hill.

Russ Hill was probably Owen's age, maybe a little older, and had the kind of All American good looks that made people very surprised when a man turned out to be a serial killer. Not that Hill was a serial killer.

Probably not.

But he captured Owen's attention, and Owen still didn't know why. Had they served together? Gone to school together? Rode the subway together? His mind was caught on the puzzle, which only had him half listening to Peters as he went over the protocols Stasia was supposed to be following.

"You'll liaise with me during core hours," Peters was telling them, "and then Rivera or Griffin during their shifts. Any questions?"

Stasia sat at her desk and leaned back in the chair, thinking for a moment before shaking her head. "I appreciate that you're here to help me. I'll try to make this as painless as possible for you."

That would have startled a sound out of Owen if he wasn't still snagged on Hill. He didn't like that guy and he couldn't put his finger on why. But since Stasia had no questions, the meeting was over. The surveillance team got up and started filing out of the room.

Did Owen need to bring up his uneasiness about Hill? Or was he on high alert and overreacting?

Hill made it to the door and looked over his shoulder, his face half-obscured by one of the room's deep shadows. Seeing him like that was enough to trigger a dark memory in Owen, one he would never be able to forget.

How could a person forget the night their life changed forever?

Dense forest. Denser shadows. Torches flickering in a slight breeze, barely illuminating the clearing around them. It was like something out of an ancient fairy tale. The Black Forest, evil magic, scary sigils dug into old trees, and the scent of decay in the air.

One moment Owen had been heading back to base, the next he awoke, bound with thick rope and barely able to move.

There was red paint—he hoped it was paint—all over his naked arms and chest, and the wooden slab under him felt worn from years of use.

At first he could barely make out the forms at the edge of the light, and then he was certain they were demons sent to drag him to hell. Owen had never been more than casually religious. Until now. Now he would pray to every saint to save him.

But no one was coming.

In the shadows, he saw a form wearing a giant animal's pelt, head and all, like a robe. There were other fur clad figures, but interspersed with them were normal looking people, men and women in fatigues holding guns.

The flashback let Owen out and he jerked in his seat, barely managing to hold in his gasp.

"Are you alright?" Stasia asked.

"Fine." How was he supposed to answer that? *I think one of your surveillance team kidnapped me two years ago and turned me into a werewolf.* Yeah, not happening. Already he was beginning to doubt the memory. Why would Russ Hill have been there? And why would a guy who had something to do with secret German werewolf rituals be guarding an heiress in New York?

Then again, anyone could ask why a werewolf was guarding a New York heiress. All Owen could tell them was that the job market was weird.

"Did you know your security detail before today?" He wasn't willing to dismiss that memory as fantasy. Just because he couldn't think of a reason why Hill would have been in Germany didn't mean there wasn't one.

She shook her head. "No, they're my father's people. Should I be concerned?"

"No. I'm sure it's fine." He had to think more before he said anything about Hill. Accusing him without more information could open up a can of worms he wasn't ready to deal with.

He probably needed to talk to Gibson.

But Stasia had her teeth in it and didn't want to let go. "Is it? You look like you've seen a ghost."

Of course she was the type that couldn't let a thing like that go. But he didn't want her focusing on it, and he certainly couldn't explain werewolves. Not yet. Not to her.

It was time to change the subject. "What did your brother mean when he said Bermeja? That's in the Caribbean, right? My file says you lived there for a bit. What were you, some resort doctor or something? Living it up?"

She pushed up from her chair and took a step towards him, gray eyes fiery with indignation. "Excuse me?"

He'd said something wrong. He could feel it. But

there was no backing out now. And a part of him wanted to see how she would fight. She seemed like a good sparring partner. "Your brother said something happened to you in Bermeja." He pushed off the wall he'd been leaning on and stalked closer to her.

She didn't back down. If anything, his presence fueled her fire. "I was almost kidnapped, but they didn't get as close as the guy got yesterday." She said it with the kind of detachment that came after reciting a terrible story over and over again. "And I was providing medical support after one of the island's hospitals was destroyed after Hurricane Charles a few years ago. Not much time to sip Mai Tais on the beach, I'm afraid."

"Oh." He should have read the file closer. And he should have read it again after meeting her. Nothing about the woman he'd been following all day matched with the picture he'd drawn in his head. He needed to stop judging her against what he expected.

But now Stasia was on a roll. "I get it. You think I'm some spoiled princess with too much money and a daddy ready to sweep in and solve every problem."

She was spoiling for a fight, and the shock of seeing Hill, of that flashback, was still fresh in his mind, keeping him on edge. Owen knew he should deescalate, but he was right on the edge and he wanted more.

He ran his hand over the cherry wood of one of the shelves. "This house sure says so. What's it cost? Three, four million?" He shared a place with Andre out in Queens, and even there the rent was disgusting.

She shook her head. "I'm not defending myself to you."

Somehow they'd ended up standing close together. All Owen had to do was reach out and pull her body flush with his before he covered her mouth with his lips and gave her the searing kiss she deserved.

She was thinking the same thing. Her eyes flicked down to his lips and then back up to meet his. Was that a dare he saw? Or was he aching too much to read this right?

His wolf whimpered and scratched inside of his skin, begging him to take her, to make her his. He wanted her wearing his mark, wanted everyone to know that she belonged to him. It was primal and possessive and nothing like Owen had ever felt before.

It terrified him, and yet he couldn't back away from it.

Stasia held a hand up, just an inch away from his

chest. He leaned in against it and could feel his heart pounding against her palm.

Her tongue darted out and wet her lips. This was happening. Nothing in the world was strong enough to tear them apart.

Nothing except for the good doctor herself.

She jerked her hand away and took two steps so she was half out the library door. "I'm in for the night. No more running away. You can sleep in the guest room."

She was running away. She could feel the heat pounding between them. She wanted him as much as he wanted her. But she was running.

And his wolf was eager for the chase.

CHAPTER EIGHT

WAS she out of her goddamn mind? In the hour since the meeting with her security detail, Stasia had been hiding in her room. She could pretend it was because it was the most secure room in her house, but she wasn't sure that was accurate. And it definitely wasn't true.

She was hiding from Owen.

She could still feel the heat of his body on her hand, the imprint of his skin and muscles, even if there had been his shirt between them. And now all she could imagine was what it would feel like if that shirt wasn't there. Would he be as toned as she imagined? Would he have chest hair for her fingers to play in? Or would he be all smooth and sleek?

Thinking about it was going to drive her nuts. It was all just hormones and pent up horniness. She hadn't been laid since... oh god, she couldn't remember the last time she had sex. She wasn't exactly the cuddly type and relationships didn't come easy. And one night stands? No, thanks. She needed to know her bed partners.

She didn't know Owen, but that didn't seem to matter to her brain... or her lady bits.

The shower turned on, and she could imagine what Owen looked like all naked under the hot spray. But she wasn't going to. He was her employee. That was creepy. There was a power dynamic that couldn't be avoided.

And *that* was a steaming pile of bullshit excuses that Stasia was certain would dissolve the next time she laid eyes on him.

But with Owen in the shower, it meant she could sneak downstairs without the risk of seeing him.

That was good. If he could be her invisible shadow for the next week, that would be absolutely fucking *peachy*. Her life was spinning out of control and so were her hormones, and she needed to get control of something.

Dinner. Dinner was something she could control.

She felt like a prisoner in her own house when she paused at the door to her bedroom and listened carefully to make sure the water was still running. It was. She hoped Owen liked long showers. She wouldn't even begrudge him the hot water.

Had she really touched him like that?

Had they really almost kissed?

Stasia couldn't put it out of her mind, and she kept flexing her hand involuntarily, as if that would make the memory of his body go away.

There were plenty of stories of women she knew getting tangled up in affairs with their bodyguards. It wasn't exactly unheard of. But it felt so stereotypical. Poor little rich girl gets threatened. Big, strong, sexy man swoops in to protect her. They fall into bed together and end up with a bunch of messy emotions.

No thanks.

She ate some leftovers and tried to put Owen out of her mind, even as it occurred to her that she would need to feed the man. She pulled a pad of Post-Its out of a drawer and stuck one on the fridge after instructing Owen to eat anything he wanted.

Host duties taken care of, she sat at her small kitchen table and contemplated what to do for the rest of the week. She had two more volunteer shifts at the clinic scheduled, but she couldn't bring her bullshit there. She tapped out an email to her supervisor and let her know she wasn't coming in this week.

There. Schedule cleared.

How sad was that?

Luna already expected not to see her and she couldn't think of any other friends she needed to call. And what about her siblings? They barely saw each other as it was. The only one she saw with any regularity, other than AR, was Emerald, but her younger sister was probably in some far flung city living it up right now.

Stasia cleaned up after herself and listened, satisfied that the water was still running. She could sneak back upstairs.

She hated that she was hiding, and she regretted promising not to run away again. But she had to be a big girl and deal with it. He was staying in her house; that meant they would see each other.

Stasia took some deep breaths to steady herself. A little bit of lust was nothing. Seriously. She just had to put thoughts of Owen aside and deal with it.

But as she walked up the steps, she realized the water had stopped running. She tried to tell herself it didn't matter. He was in the bathroom, she didn't need to see him.

The bathroom door was open.

Owen stood in front of the mirror, towel hanging precariously around his hips.

Stasia stopped in her tracks. She didn't mean to.

She knew the right thing to do was to keep moving. But no power in the universe could have forced her forward at that moment.

Rivulets of water dripped from his dark hair and traced a path over his muscles and the light dusting of hair on his glistening chest. Her tongue curled up in her mouth, straining and desperate to lick that water up.

Owen turned and caught her staring, his mouth pulling up into a wolfish grin. Had his teeth always been that sharp? And when had his eyes turned yellow? Weren't they brown?

She was so far away that she shouldn't have been able to see his eyes, but that didn't matter at the moment. Stasia felt trapped, prey stunned by a predator, with no chance of escape. It was crazy. Intense. Too much.

"Enjoy the view?" Owen asked. He used a hand towel to wipe at his chest, and Stasia had to bite the inside of her cheek to keep from reacting. Heat coiled deep within her and she wanted to get close, wanted Owen to soothe the ache he was causing.

She needed to take control of this situation. She wasn't going to jump Owen's bones, and it would be easier to hold true to that vow if she wasn't looking at him. "Can't you keep the door closed?" Seriously? *That* was her brilliant response?

Owen chuckled darkly, and it felt like a caress against her most private places. If he could do that with a sound, she was terrified to think of what he could do if he got his hands on her.

"Do you need to shower?" he asked. He tilted his head back, as if inviting her into the bathroom with him, inviting her to join him in the shower.

"I have my own." And she had to cling to that. She wasn't going to do anything with Owen. He was in her house to protect her, not get in her pants. She wasn't going to cross that line. It wasn't fair to him.

No matter how much her body was screaming at her to act.

"I'd be happy to help." The wolfish grin got even more predatory. It would have scared her if it wasn't so sexy. "It's my job to keep you safe."

Somehow his reminder was the bucket of ice she needed, even if the reminders she'd been thinking to herself did nothing. Owen was her bodyguard. He was doing his job. His job was not to be her gigolo.

"There's food in the kitchen," she muttered before scampering to her room.

She hated that she kept running from him, but she was afraid to find out what would happen the moment she stopped.

CHAPTER NINE

OWEN BREATHED deep as he watched Stasia walk away. The need to chase her pounded in his heart, and he had to grip his towel tight to keep from taking off, as if that was strong enough to root him in place.

His wolf wanted to tear out of his skin and tackle her, take her, claim her until she understood that she was *his*. And he didn't know how to deal with that. Since when did his wolf care about the women he wanted?

Mate.

The word was rough, not quite human, and it definitely didn't sound like Owen. He wasn't sure if he'd said it out loud or in his mind, but it rattled around, a concept too big for him to ignore. He'd tried to do research on werewolves, but his options were limited. Still, Owen had come across the word before. Was it real? Was it possible?

If his wolf had anything to say about it, it was. But Owen wasn't convinced his "wolf" was anything more than his imagination trying to deal with something outside of his normal. He was an easy going guy. He didn't get possessive, especially not for a princess who he was only going to be around for a week.

And what kind of stunt was that? Preening in front of her in just a towel? Throwing out sexual comments like he had a right? She could fire him for that and he would deserve it.

He had to get control.

Owen slammed the door and winced at the sound it made against the old wood of her house. He wasn't supposed to have super strength, but he was beginning to think he knew exactly jack shit about what it meant to be a werewolf.

He gripped the edges of the porcelain vanity and breathed deep, trying to center himself. He raised his head up and looked in the mirror.

His eyes were wolfish, shifted to a golden tone far different from his normal brown. Owen squeezed his eyes shut and looked again, as if that would banish it. But no, they were still gold. He opened his mouth to check his teeth. Were they extra sharp? He wasn't sure.

And that was another problem. Wolf and man were binary states. He was a man. He was a wolf. There wasn't an in between, except for in the moments of the shift. One of the first things he and his fellow wolves had tried to do when they first shifted was summon claws like they were comic book characters.

It hadn't worked. All Owen got for his efforts was a headache.

Maybe they'd started too big.

But Owen didn't want claws now. He closed his eyes once more and concentrated on his humanity. He breathed deep and thought human thoughts: thumbs, beer, church. No wolf had ever been dragged to Sunday School.

It worked. When he opened his eyes they were a reassuring brown once more, and his teeth looked like teeth.

Crisis averted, Owen dried off as quickly as possible, doing his best to ignore his cock. He had to. His job depended on it.

And possibly his humanity.

Did he need to apologize to Stasia?

Owen wasn't sure what she would want, and he

didn't want to make things worse. She'd almost kissed him in the library, he was certain of it.

Or maybe that was his wolf seeing things he wanted to see.

He'd play it by ear. And he'd behave. No more funny business.

Of course, his resolve was tested the moment he stepped out of the bathroom. His wolf tugged him towards Stasia's closed door, but Owen resisted, fighting against the force until he was safely ensconced in his own bedroom.

It wasn't much: a queen bed, a wardrobe, and a small window that looked out onto the park. Way more peaceful than anything in his apartment. He could barely hear any noise from the city. He could almost pretend he was back on Gibson's farm.

And maybe Gibson was exactly who he needed. Owen pulled out his phone and dialed.

"Is something wrong?" Gibson barked out as soon as the call connected.

Owen scrunched his brow. "Wrong? Why?" He needed advice, he called Gibson, that was how this thing worked. Gibson was his… boss. They shied away from the other word all the werewolf fiction used.

"You already checked in."

"That was a few hours ago. I'm calling to let you

know that we worked out a rotation with the surveillance team and the client has agreed to the surveillance for one week." Now that he was talking, he wondered if he really needed to talk about the rest of it. He'd had a moment of crazy. It happened to everyone. Really, he was feeling fine now.

But Gibson had some magic power to sense when Owen was avoiding things. "I know all that. What's going on, Myers?"

It felt weird to bring it up. Gibson was like the dad of their little group, and Owen had never talked to his parents about sex. They were a good Catholic family. They ignored that shit until it blew up in their faces, just like God intended. He was pretty sure his parents still thought he was a virgin.

But Gibson hasn't his dad. He had to tell him. "My wolf feels weird." They all reported strange werewolf bullshit to Gibson when it happened.

"Your wolf? What does that mean?" There wasn't any judgment, just confusion.

"You know what I mean, man. The hairy dude inside of me. Four legs. Howls at the moon." Owen realized he might have been talking loud enough for Stasia to hear and lowered his voice. He did *not* want his ma—his client to overhear this conversation.

"You think of it as a separate entity?" He could

imagine Gibson noting this whole thing down on a clipboard like Owen was a fascinating specimen.

"Not usually. But today it's really feeling like it. Is that normal?" He hoped Gibson had answers. It wasn't like the major had more werewolfing experience than the rest of them, but sometimes it felt like it. He had that kind of presence.

Gibson huffed out a laugh. "We're werewolves. We left normal behind a long time ago."

"There's something about…" He didn't want to say Stasia's name. His wolf wanted to guard her viciously and keep anyone from her. She was *his*. But he'd only known her for a day. What if Gibson could explain what was going on? What if he could fix it?

"About what?"

He had to say it. She was his client. Gibson was his boss. And he wasn't going to lie to him. "The client. Stasia… um… Dr. Nichols." They didn't generally get on a first name basis with their clients, and Owen hoped his slip up wasn't that noticeable.

Apparently it wasn't. Sometimes it paid off to be a bit too cheery and informal. "What about her?"

How was he supposed to explain it? He couldn't even explain it to himself, and he was sitting in his own brain. "My wolf… I… She's very attractive."

"She's not the first hot woman you've needed to protect. Is this something else?" There was something in Gibson's voice that made Owen leery, like Gibson knew something Owen didn't and he hadn't told. For some reason.

"I don't know." He tried to think back to his other clients, but everyone paled in comparison to Stasia. They might as well have never existed.

"Do you need to be taken off of this detail?"

His wolf flared to life inside of him at the thought. Give up Stasia? Never. "No," he snarled.

"Myers," Gibson warned, a bit of his own wolf's rumble coming through.

It was enough to make Owen take a breath. "I'm okay. I promise." He'd never snarled at Gibson—or *anyone*—before, especially not in human form. That had to be bad. What was so special about Stasia? Why couldn't he control himself?

Gibson took him at his word. "Contact me if anything changes. We need to keep track of what our wolves are doing. We're the only werewolves in the universe. There isn't a rulebook for this."

That was true. *Teen Wolf* hadn't done much to teach Owen about what it meant to be wolfy. Gibson disconnected, and Owen realized he'd been so caught up in his emotions about Stasia that he forgot to say anything about Hill.

Fuck.

He considered calling Gibson back, but stopped

himself. He had no proof that Hill had been there that night. All he had was half a memory and a sense of foreboding. With his wolf going haywire, he didn't want to give Gibson more cause for worry.

Were they the only werewolves in existence?

His mind snagged on what Gibson said, and he had to wonder. They'd been turned into werewolves deliberately… for some reason. Presumably whoever had done the turning knew it would happen. So was that the first time? Or were there other groups of people running around thinking *they* were the only werewolves on the planet?

And what if there were werewolves that weren't created by magic? None of the books and TV shows worked that way. Were werewolf bites contagious? They'd all wondered, but there was no ethical way to test it out.

Focusing on the mysteries of his existence would drive him crazier than his desire for Stasia. But he needed answers about at least one of the mysteries of his life, or he feared his wolf would tear out of his skin and start looking for answers himself.

CHAPTER TEN

STASIA HAD to stop thinking about Owen in the sexy way. Her body was hornier than ever, and her mind kept concocting schemes to make it okay to have her way with him. She didn't do things like that. She didn't *think* things like that.

And yet she'd woken up panting—twice!—while in the middle of dreaming about what Owen could do to her.

That man looked like he had a wicked tongue and she wanted to find out if it was true.

She had to forget about those dreams and lingual speculation. He was her employee, her bodyguard, even if she wasn't paying for him, and she wasn't going to take advantage. She wasn't sure how many times she had to tell herself that to make the resolve stick. Ten thousand? Maybe the number didn't exist.

She was screwed.

And not by Owen.

She spent her morning doing her best to ignore him. The morning began with yoga and a healthy breakfast and ignoring that Owen was right down the hall. After breakfast she looked over some papers that her accountant had sent her regarding the month's charitable donations.

And then she ran out of stuff to do.

Stasia hated being bored. She thrived in the emergency room, the chaos of hurt and healing circling her. On a morning like this, she could kick herself for leaving her last hospital. It had sounded all noble, sacrificing her position rather than lose another doctor or some nurses to budget cuts.

But she needed to figure out what to do next.

Surely some other emergency room in the city needed a doctor. Not that she was going to apply when someone was trying to kidnap her. But it was time to start getting her name out there again.

Even if she wasn't sure that was what she wanted to do with her life.

That was the part about quitting she didn't think of too much. Yes, she thrived in the chaos, but she hated hospital politics. Sacrificing her job to save another person's paycheck hadn't been an entirely selfless act.

But what were her other options? Private practice? Another humanitarian trip? Med school had not prepared her for this career crisis.

Or maybe she had ignored any help there was to offer. Her father *had* always called her too independent for her own good.

Leaving her office meant seeing Owen, but thinking about the future of her career was enough to drive her crazy. She'd rather deal with the bodyguard at the moment.

Her house was big by New York standards, but that didn't actually make it large. Every time she stepped out of a room, Owen was there. Sure, it was his job, but that didn't make it any less annoying.

Why had she agreed to this?

She tidied up for a little while. Normally she had someone come in and clean once a week, but that was another thing that had needed to be canceled once she was in danger. She trusted the service she hired, but it was such an obvious infiltration point that she'd canceled this week's service before Owen even showed up. She wasn't completely oblivious to the trouble that was following her.

But Stasia was already relatively neat, and there wasn't much to tidy. And Owen was *right there.*

She gave up. There was no ignoring him, and she couldn't make tasks appear out of thin air. She turned to Owen, who was sitting on one of the library couches. "Want to watch something?" She picked up the remote and pressed the button to open the cabinet where her TV was discreetly tucked away.

He jerked in surprise at her acknowledgement. "I thought you were coming in here to read."

Stasia felt strangely defensive. "I watch TV. I'm a normal person."

Owen tilted his head to the side and gave her an assessing look. "I've never met a normal person like you before."

"What's that supposed to mean?" Stasia sat down on the other side of the couch. She didn't want to sit next to him if he was going to be mean, but she did want to look at the screen.

He flicked his items off on his fingers. "Billionaire dad. Nine half-siblings. *Actual* career despite being a rich girl. Humanitarian mission. Should I keep going?"

She couldn't tell if he was trying to insult or compliment her. If she didn't have the day before to go on, she would have taken the last bits for compliments. She didn't know how to handle him if he was going to be nice. She could handle their antagonistic banter. But her knees would go weak if he turned out to be decent.

And she was trying to ignore her feelings.

Owen smiled as she kept quiet and his eyes started to sparkle. Was he really so cheerful? Had she read him wrong? It would be easy enough to ignore. All Stasia had to do was turn on the TV and end the conversation.

But she couldn't. "So what's your story? You don't seem like a bodyguard." Every bodyguard she'd ever employed was all business, all the time. A good trait in someone trying to keep her safe, but not exactly memorable. There was something about Owen, though, something that made her want him physically *and* sit down beside him to watch TV.

He blew out a breath and grimaced. "That was *not* the plan."

Wasn't that how life went? But now that she had a taste, she wanted to know more. "I know a thing or two about plans changing. What was yours? Originally?"

He laid his arm on the back of the sofa and ran his fingers over the red leather. Some part of him always seemed to be in motion. "Army for a while. I didn't really think much past that."

She looked at him, *really* looked at him, and tried to imagine him in fatigues on a battlefield somewhere. It didn't fit. "Full career?" Then again, she didn't always seem to fit in the places she wanted to be.

But he shook his head. "I wasn't going to go that far."

Stasia turned more fully to him and placed the remote on the side table. "How long have you been out?"

A dark look passed over his face so quickly that she wasn't sure she really saw it. "Two years."

"Doesn't sound like you planned it." But maybe Owen wasn't a planner, maybe he just let things happen.

"I didn't."

"Want to tell me what happened?" Now that she was asking, she was desperate to know. She could feel a secret hiding beneath the surface and she wanted to cut it away, layer by layer, until she knew it all.

He waggled his eyebrows and grinned. "I'd tell you but then I would have to kill you."

"I thought you were supposed to protect me."

He made a rumbly sound in the back of his throat that did things to Stasia, things she wasn't allowed to think about. Danger! Danger! She threw another question out there, desperate for a lifeline out of flirty territory. "Do you like New York? Do you even live in New York regularly?"

His finger dipped into one of the divots on the couch and circled around one of the decorative buttons. Stasia tried not to imagine what his fingers would feel like against her skin. "The company is based out of New York. I live in Queens. Raised in Jersey. It's alright."

Alright. Some people said New York was the greatest city in the world. Stasia agreed with Owen's assessment. It was fine. It was where she lived. But just like with the future of her career, she wasn't sure it was where she wanted to stay.

"What made you want to go to Bermeja?" Owen asked.

The question caught her off guard. Her father and AR had railed at her, demanding she not go. Em had insisted that she needed to go, just to stick it to them. But no one had wanted to know why. "I saw the devastation of Hurricane Charles and I knew I had to help. I always wanted to go into emergency medicine and I wanted to go someplace that really needed help. The dirty secret of a lot of humanitarian missions is that they need people with money to make things work. I had all the qualifications and I have the bank account where I could afford to do it. So I went. And as crazy, as hard, as terrible as the conditions were, I loved doing it. Helping people like that. I felt almost like I was made to do it."

"What do you mean by that?" He was leaning closer, as if her story had pulled him in.

Stasia could practically feel the grit in the air from the makeshift hospital she'd been working in. Reconstruction never seemed to end and a fine sheen of dust had covered every surface. "Thinking on my feet. Improvising. Just making it work. It really made me test my abilities to the furthest limits of what I learned and to listen to people who didn't go to a super fancy med school that had every single piece of technology that a person could ever hope for."

The scent memory of the place was obliterated by the smell of Owen's soap. When had he gotten so close? Had *she* moved closer? She must have; they were both leaning towards the middle of the couch, pulled together as if they were stuck in each other's gravitational orbits.

"What about the other doctors?" he asked, his fingers close enough to touch her if he stretched a little. "You meet a cute humanitarian who wanted to save the world with you?"

Stasia could barely imagine that. "We were way too busy for that. And, well. I'm me." She'd managed to make exactly one friend in her entire medical career, and that friend was about to abandon her to another job.

Owen's face scrunched in confusion and the tips of his fingers teased her shoulder. "What's that supposed to mean?"

It was her turn for confusion. What was there to explain? He'd only been around her for a day, but he had to know, right? People didn't get close to her, and those who tried quickly retreated when they realized there wasn't some secret soft core under her prickly skin. "I'm a bit abrasive."

He stared at her in a way that felt like a caress, and then his hand moved, almost like he planned to touch her face. She wanted him to. She wanted him to reach out and close the distance between them, to put an end to this dance and quench the thirst she'd had for him since the moment she laid eyes on him. But he stopped his hand before he reached her.

Stasia was done fighting. She was done worrying about whether it was appropriate or not. She laid her head in his hand and let his fingers stroke her cheek, her eyes falling closed at the sensation.

"I don't think you're abrasive. I think you're kind of amazing." There was reverence in his tone, something she'd never heard another say about her, and her heart pounded wildly.

She opened her eyes and stared right into his. Brown now, soft and promising. When they'd appeared gold last night it must have been a trick of the light. Possibility hung heavy in the air. All it would take was for one of them to make a move.

One of them did.

Maybe both.

Stasia wasn't sure, and then Owen was kissing her and she didn't care. His hand cradled the back of her head, holding her close to him like she was precious. Her hands went to his shoulders, fingers digging into hard muscle and clinging desperately, begging him with her touch not to pull away.

He groaned deep in his throat and heat curled inside Stasia. She moved forward until she straddled his lap, fully on top of him and still desperate for more contact. It was carnal, feral, something *more* than she'd ever felt before.

It should have scared her, this roaring inferno of need, but Owen was touching her, kissing her, and fear had no place here, not between the two of them.

His tongue swiped against hers and it was her turn to groan. Talented tongue. She knew it and she wanted more. What could he do if she had him in bed?

A faint ringing interrupted them and Stasia was confused. Then Owen stiffened under her and pulled away. His pupils were huge and his lips swollen. He looked at her with unquenchable heat, and Stasia wanted to lean right in and ignore whoever was trying to interrupt them. She didn't think any man had ever looked at her like that.

"Phone," Owen said, voice gone gravelly with lust. "Could be important."

"Probably isn't." She would have ignored just about anything if it meant he would kiss her again.

But Owen was still her bodyguard and he still took the job seriously, even when his hard cock was trapped between them.

He answered the phone and Stasia was impressed with how professional he sounded. A wicked, newly awakened part of her wanted to play with him, to kiss and touch and see how long it would take his demeanor to break.

But that wasn't her. She didn't do things like that. Instead she slid off of him and ran her fingers through her hair, trying to get it into something approaching order.

Someone knocked at the door.

Stasia looked down the hall as if that would reveal who it was. She wasn't expecting anyone, but trusted the doorman not to let a stranger come up. Owen was still speaking quietly into the phone so she stood, planning to check the security camera.

His hand flashed out and he grabbed her wrist. "I'm going with you. Don't answer the door."

A cascade of emotions slammed through her: frustration that he thought she was stupid enough to blindly open the door, fear that someone had gotten past the doorman, a stubborn desire to actually answer the door just to spite him, and a bit of residual lust at his commanding tone.

She wasn't going to examine that last one too closely.

The knocking stopped.

Owen ended his call and put his phone down. "Surveillance was checking in, they saw someone head up."

"I'm not expecting anyone." Stasia's brain was still a bit frazzled from the kiss and it took her a moment to get her thoughts in order.

Owen stood up right next to her, the concept of personal space forgotten. "Does anyone have a key? I thought you said you didn't have a boyfriend."

A boyfriend? What did he mean by that? Why would he care? Well… maybe he had reason. Was he jealous?

Footsteps tapped down the hallway and Owen stepped in front of her. Whoever it was clearly did have a key, and there were only a few people Stasia trusted that much.

A blonde woman stepped in the doorway to the library and looked at Owen and then over his shoulder to Stasia. "Am I interrupting something?" her sister, Emerald, asked.

CHAPTER ELEVEN

EMERALD SELBY LOOKED A LITTLE FAMILIAR, but Owen wasn't sure why. Was it a resemblance to Stasia? There might have been a hint of it in the curve of her jaw and the shape of her nose, but with blonde hair falling in gentle waves past her shoulders and eyes as blue as the sea, not much about her coloring suggested a connection.

Some survival instinct instructed him to put distance between himself and his client. His wolf protested, but he managed to take half a step. He could still taste her on his lips and remember the press of her body as she sat in his lap.

He was going to kiss her again. And when he did, they weren't going to be interrupted.

His body ached with want. He knew lust. He'd been a horny asshole at times, but it was nothing like what he felt when it came to her. His wolf was unsettled in his skin. He wanted Stasia's sister to go away so he and Stasia could get back to what they were meant to be doing.

Mate.

There was that word again. If he thought it a few more times, he wondered if he'd begin to believe it. Was something like that possible? Was she his?

Yes.

His wolf knew it, even if the man was still trying to figure a thing or two out. But he knew that a person didn't forget a kiss like that, and they didn't let go of a woman like Stasia.

He wasn't supposed to get attached to his clients. Gibson would probably have kittens if he knew what Owen wanted. Damn the consequences, Owen was ready to take on the world for the chance to stand at Stasia's side.

If she would give him that chance.

Emerald came further into the library and pulled a small rolling suitcase in behind her. It was one of those hard cased suitcases in a blinding red.

"Fuck," said Stasia, stepping around Owen to get closer to her sister. She looked at the suitcase and then back up at Emerald, as if she hoped they might magically disappear.

Emerald crossed her arms. "You forgot?"

"What's going on?" He and Stasia had gone over her plans for the week and she'd failed to mention this visit. From his standpoint as a guard, it wasn't a huge deal. Emerald was a trusted family member and if she had ill will towards Stasia she wouldn't need to have her abducted off the street, she had a key to the woman's house. But from the perspective of Owen's cock? Not great.

Stasia gave her sister a half hug. "I'm sorry, Em. Some shit's gone down. I guess AR didn't loop you in. It's probably best if you just get a hotel." She winced as she suggested it, and Owen wondered why. There wasn't a hotel in the city they couldn't afford—even if they wanted to buy the building outright rather than just rent a room—and no doubt Em wouldn't want to be caught in the line of fire if something went down.

Not that Owen would let either of them get hurt.

Em was shaking her head, eyes wide and stubborn. "You know what happens when I go to hotels." She grimaced. "It's so much better if I stay with you..." There was a pause. "Unless this is sex week that I'm interrupting."

"No!" Stasia stepped to the other side of Em, putting as much distance as possible between herself and Owen.

That stung a little. A sex week sounded like a

dream. But he found it almost… cute, the way Stasia jumped right there. From some other woman he might have seen it as a rejection, but not from Stasia. Maybe it was just his wolf engaging in wishful thinking.

Or maybe this was more than just lust.

Mate.

Em looked between him and Stasia, eyes raised and skeptical. "I mean, I guess I could stay at Dad's penthouse. As long as Riley isn't there." She sounded even less enthusiastic than the idea of the hotel.

"Riley is one of your sisters?" Owen asked. There was a whole family tree in Stasia's file, but it was convoluted and he was bad at remembering names. He vaguely remembered a Riley.

Em scoffed. "She's our twenty-three-year-old stepmother."

Yikes. Owen didn't know how to react to that. He knew Stasia was thirty-four and Em looked like she was in her late twenties. It was no secret that Armand Selby had been married several times, but Owen had never paid attention to the ages of his wives. He was curious to know how Stasia felt about that, but now was not the time to ask. Clearly Em wasn't a fan.

"You have to get over it eventually," said Stasia.

"Why?" Em finally gave up on standing in the

doorway and came all the way in and leaned on Stasia's desk. From the ease of the movement, Owen had no doubt she'd done it a hundred times before. "It's not like she's going to last for long. Name stealer."

"What?" The more Em talked, the less Owen understood. What was with this family? He thought being a werewolf made him weird, but it had nothing on the weirdness of the outrageously wealthy.

Neither sister answered him. "I won't make you stay at Dad's," said Stasia. "You can stay here. Owen is my bodyguard. There was a kidnapping attempt the other day. Dad and AR insisted on a babysitter. Just for the week. They don't think it'll take long to figure stuff out." She didn't look at him while she explained the situation.

Owen didn't like the reminder of the time limit. But a week—six days now—was plenty of time. Not to get her out of his system. One kiss was enough to know that wouldn't happen. But all he had to do was convince her to take a shot on him.

Surely she'd want to upgrade her werewolf bodyguard to werewolf boyfriend.

Right?

Em's eyes got wide, this time in surprise. "Another kidnapping attempt? Why do they always come for you?"

It sounded offensive, but Stasia smiled. "I'm an easy target. Shouldn't you have hulking men surrounding you at this point?"

Em shook her head. "I gave them the week off. I just need a week to be a normal person. Or a few days. I guess your bodyguard will have to be eye candy enough." Owen was a bit lost on why Em needed bodyguards, and he wondered if it had something to do with why she looked so familiar. But he couldn't resist preening a bit when she objectified him.

"Keep your hands to yourself." The words were jealous and petty out of Stasia's mouth and Owen's eyes got wide. Maybe he was closer to werewolf boyfriend status than he thought.

"Oooooooh. What have we got here?" Em pushed off the desk and stepped close to her sister, grinning from ear to ear at the idea of Stasia's possessiveness of Owen.

He loved listening to the banter, but he knew when to make his exit. The sisters needed time to reminisce, and they couldn't do it properly if he was standing right there. "I'll let you two get caught up," he said.

But as he left the room, he trailed a hand down Stasia's arm, a reminder that the thing between them was far from over.

CHAPTER TWELVE

Stasia could still feel Owen's touch as she went back to the couch and sat down. She patted the seat next to her for Em to join her, her cheeks warm. She expected him to do the normal thing: ignore everything they'd just done together and let things go back to normal.

She was going to tuck that kiss deep into her memory and revisit it every time she needed a pick me up. But she could barely dream of letting it be more. What was she to Owen? What was he to her?

What could they become?

Everything. The instinct was terrifying and exhilarating, and she was almost sure it was right. If she let him, if she wanted, they could be everything together.

With one casual touch, he'd destroyed her

expectations, and she was excited to see just how he planned to build them up again. Owen wasn't like any man she'd ever dated, ever kissed. And if he got under her skin, she didn't know that she'd be able to let him go.

Who was she kidding? He was under her skin already.

Em sank down onto the couch next to her and gave her a bright, questioning look. "What's going on? You're grinning."

"Nothing's going on." Stasia bristled. Sure, she was having happy thoughts about Owen; it didn't mean she wanted Em to come in and make it weird.

But Em had the instincts of a little sister and she wasn't about to drop it. "You keep touching your lips. Those pillows over there are way more messed up than you would ever allow. And that guy looked at you like he was thinking naughty thoughts and you didn't do anything to tell them off. So what's going on between the two of you? Bodyguard?" she scoffed. "Yeah, right."

"He *is* my bodyguard. We just also kissed a little bit." Stasia blushed even deeper as she admitted it. What was the point in hiding it? Em could have been Sherlock Holmes if her music career hadn't taken off.

"Oh my God!" She bounced up and down on the

cushion in excitement. "I didn't know you had it in you."

"Shut up." She wanted to swear Em to secrecy, but that was likely to have the story spread around the family out of spite. Em was eight years and two marriages younger than Stasia, and they'd only gotten close when Stasia lived in the same property as Em while she was in med school and Em in high school. Out of all her siblings, she was closest to Em, and she only saw the others on rare occasions when the lawyers pulled them together or there was a big gathering.

That reminded her. "Are you going to the birthday party?" It was a bit evil to ask, and the grin she had from kissing Owen turned into the kind of maniacal smile only an older sister could give.

"I hate you," Em scowled.

Score one for Stasia. "You love me."

It was enough to set Em off *and* to have her stop asking about Owen. Win-win as far as Stasia was concerned. "She stole my name. There is room for one Emerald Selby in this family and it's me. She can change the baby's name and then I'll go meet it."

Stasia winced at "it." "I think you're going a little too far." She didn't need to play peacemaker, but she didn't want her sister stuck in a grudge forever.

"I'm not going far enough." Em's scowl got even

darker, like she was planning something vile for Riley.

"It's a baby. And it's not the baby's fault." They'd been over this conversation any time the family came up in the last three years, and Stasia had her part memorized by now.

"Doesn't it have a middle name it can go by?"

"I think you're being more childish than Riley. You can't force her to change the name now. When the baby's old enough maybe she'll want to go by something else. Just like you do." Stasia and the family were just about the only people who called Em by her name; even Riley usually referred to her by her stage name, Mercy. Naming the kids was up to his wives, and that little misunderstanding was how their father ended up with two daughters named Emerald.

Em deflated since Stasia wasn't commiserating enough. "Are *you* going to the birthday party?"

She might have been the only Stasia in the family, but that didn't mean she wanted to go to a toddler's shindig. "I'm trying to claim attempted kidnapping. AR doesn't want to buy it. If I can avoid it I will."

Em scrunched up her face. "Are we terrible?"

"We might be." But Stasia was pretty sure it was normal to want to avoid family occasions. Every movie and TV show about normal families seemed to have some sort of plot revolving around it. The Selbys weren't normal, but they could fake it.

Em grew concerned and curious. "So was the kidnapping because of Dad's bullshit this time? Again?"

"Can't imagine it was anything else." Safe in her own home with her sister by her side and Owen somewhere in the building, she wasn't freaked out, she was angry. Selby Group had a finger in every pie, many of them completely illegal. The first kidnapping attempt back in Bermeja had been about ransom. Stasia didn't know if it was the same thing now or something worse. She chose not to use the Selby name to honor her mother and for the slight anonymity it gave her. Apparently it wasn't enough.

"You sound sure they'll have it taken care of."

AR had sounded confident, and Stasia was trusting him for now. "I don't want a bodyguard for the rest of my life."

"It's not as bad as it sounds," Em tried to reassure her. She normally traveled with half a dozen hulking men who kept her from the public, so it was almost strange to see her alone.

"But some of us are not in the public eye." Doctors didn't need the same protection as rock stars.

Em shrugged. "It's a living."

"Are you ready for the new tour to start?" Now

that Em was here, Stasia remembered that she was about to embark on a nationwide tour for months. This week was her last chance at anything approaching free time for awhile.

Em nodded. "I'm excited. We had a stupid delay on the album. Some of the files got corrupted on one of the masters. Had to completely re-record. But it's all fixed now and only delayed the album release by a month. But I'll be ready to start the tour soon."

"You sound happy." And Stasia was glad for it. Em had worked hard to climb to the top and Stasia couldn't wait to hear what the new music sounded like.

She shrugged. "Happy enough." She was done talking about herself. "Now dish about that Owen guy. Because if you don't want him I'll take him."

"He's mine." It came out so fast and fierce that it shocked her. Stasia was not a possessive person. She'd had a couple of boyfriends before and only one she'd call serious. *That* had ended in disaster. She had no claim to Owen, not really, but she'd fight her sister to keep him.

That got Em excited. "I knew you were going to fall for someone sometime. This is going to be good. Front row tickets."

"I know what you charge for front row tickets." Out the nose. Crazy. And the fans happily paid. "So if you want them you're going to have to pay the same price."

Em stuck her tongue out. "Like you care about money."

"I care about privacy." The thing with Owen was new and fragile and she wasn't an exhibitionist, especially not when it was her sister who was watching.

"Would it really be that bad to let someone in?" Em asked.

"I don't know. Last time I tried it didn't go so well." Her last, only, serious relationship had been back in college and med school.

"You're not over Julian? That guy sucked." Em didn't know the half of it.

Julian had wanted money and access to the Selbys more than he wanted Stasia. It had taken her way too long to figure that out. "I'm over him. It just still sometimes hurts to remember." Was there any chance Owen was like that? She knew he thought she was a spoiled rich girl, or he had, but what was under that?

"I say you give this guy a chance. Maybe he'll surprise you."

She didn't know if he was going to turn on her, but her heart was already engaged. "I don't know if I could stop myself if I wanted to."

CHAPTER THIRTEEN

OWEN WAS happy not to be banished forever. After a few hours of catching up, they invited him to share dinner and watch a movie. The best place for that was back in the library, and though the couch was more than big enough for the three of them, Em opted to sit in one of the chairs, leaving him and Stasia alone.

Could he have left space between them? Sure.

But the taste of Stasia was imprinted on Owen's memory, and he didn't want to be an inch further from her than he had to be. He didn't know if she'd kiss him again; he could barely hope for it. But sitting next to her was a good start.

He'd done a sweep of the perimeter and checked in with the surveillance team. He couldn't let his hormones get in the way of his job, and no one was getting close to Stasia on his watch.

He had to keep his mate safe.

The thought came from deep in his mind, where his wolf was prowling, demanding that he claim her, human sensibilities be damned. Owen was ignoring him. For now. He'd have to figure something else out if the wolf got more insistent.

But he was growing to like the sound of the word *mate*.

He considered checking in with Gibson, but there was no change from the day before, and he didn't need his boss thinking that he needed his hand held. He could do the job.

Stasia shivered and Owen pulled a nearby blanket over both of them. He couldn't quite read the look she gave him, and if Em's sputtering cough was anything, she saw right through his moves.

Too bad.

Andre sent him a text to let him know that the job Vega and Rowe were on was going long and they'd hit a slight snag. Apparently the happy couple hadn't made it to their honeymoon after all and needed guards for another few days. The follow up text told him not to worry.

Owen filed the information away. If Andre was updating him, it had to be at least a little serious, but it didn't sound like they needed him to abandon Stasia and this job. And it would take a lot more than a little difficulty to get him to leave her.

Where did his loyalties lie?

He knew they *should* be with his pack, the people he'd worked with for years and who'd gone through hell right alongside him. But he could feel the warmth of Stasia's body pressed against his side and he didn't know if he'd ever be able to walk away from her.

The emotions should have been scary, too intense, too fast, but Owen had never run away from emotion before, and he wasn't about to start now.

He had no idea what they were supposed to be watching. Some comedy starring actors he didn't recognize telling jokes that would probably be funnier if he was paying attention.

Instead he paid attention to the way Stasia's scent wrapped around him and the heat of her thigh.

Em said something about a canary which set Stasia off, her face open and laughing with abandon.

Owen's heartbeat kicked up at the sight. She was serious by nature, even a bit grumpy, but she'd opened up when her sister appeared and now she was all contentment. He wanted her to smile at him that way and he got a hint of it when she looked over at him, as if she was checking that he got the joke.

He couldn't have stopped the smile he gave her if he tried.

He knew her grumpy face would come back when the movie ended or when Em left, but it had its own charm. *Everything* about his brilliant doctor charmed him, and he wanted to learn all there was to know about her.

And then she shocked the living shit out of him by casually placing her hand on his leg, her fingers teasing his inner thigh, all hidden by the blanket. It wasn't an accident, not given the gentle squeeze she gave him.

Owen let out a shuddering breath. His mind might not have paid any attention, but now his cock was perking up and he was thankful that the blanket hid it all from view.

With deceptive calm, he placed his arm along the back of the sofa and slid it onto Stasia's shoulders.

Em made another noise, and if he knew her better he might have glared, but he had a feeling that things would go better for him if Stasia's sister liked him.

He wanted to trail his lips up Stasia's neck and taste her soft skin, but that was going too far and no blanket would hide the sin. He tried to think of a reason, any reason, to get Em out of the room, but it wasn't going to happen.

Stasia traced her fingers on his thigh, the small

movement driving him crazy. She was a wicked temptress.

The movie went on for longer, and Owen followed along as well as he could, laughing along with the sisters while Stasia tortured him with her fingers, at one point getting brave enough to brush up against his cock.

And then the credits began to roll and the streaming service prompted them to watch the movie's sequel.

"Do you want to keep watching?" Stasia looked over at Em as if she didn't have her fingers half an inch from Owen's balls.

Em stared at both of them like they were crazy. "Ew, no, I can practically smell the pheromones. You two are like teenagers."

Maybe that was true, but she didn't have to say it.

Stasia stiffened against him, and he feared she was going to pull away. But she didn't even move her hand when she responded. "You're just jealous I've got a hot guy."

She thought he was hot. Yeah, he liked that. A lot.

Em rolled her eyes. "I'm going to bed." She left the two of them on the couch without another word.

All alone. Finally. Now Owen could take what he'd craved all night. He leaned in, but Stasia stopped him with a hand on his chest.

"No?" Had he misread the situation?

But Stasia ran her hand up his thigh again, brushing against his cock, and he groaned, no longer worried about Em figuring out what they were doing.

Stasia nodded to the library's entrance. "My sister will pass right by the door if she needs to go downstairs." The doors were glass paneled and hid nothing. "Why don't we head to my room?"

Fuck yes. He didn't bother to ask her if she was sure. The look on her face and the feel of her hand told him that. They both wanted this, they'd wanted it for what seemed like forever, even if they'd only known each other for two days.

Two days? Two centuries? It didn't matter. Owen knew what he was feeling was real, and he wasn't going to worry about it being too fast. He only hoped she was feeling just as strongly as he was.

They let the blanket fall away as they stood, and Owen couldn't resist it, his wolf surfacing just enough to have him scooping Stasia off her feet and marching her to her room.

CHAPTER FOURTEEN

Stasia was a woman possessed.

She clung to Owen as he carried her to her room and made a sound of surprise when he slammed the door with a less than gentle kick. This wasn't her. She didn't do things like this. But when it came to Owen, there was a wild thing inside of her that demanded to be let out.

She wanted to play.

She wanted him.

And she was sick of denying herself.

Her life was going crazy. She didn't know who was after her or what the next week would bring. She couldn't count on anything, but she was going to count on this. Even if all the heat boiling between them fizzled out in the morning, she'd have tonight. She'd know what it felt like for Owen to be hers.

He let her drop down to the bed and loomed over her. Stasia stared up at him, wondering how she'd gotten so lucky.

Her whole body was tight with want, breasts heavy, sex aching to be filled. She was already wet and they'd barely done anything. Owen had cast a spell, and she never wanted it to be broken, not if it felt like this.

He was about to climb on top of her when something took hold of Stasia and she grinned. "Wait."

"What?" He didn't exactly look concerned, but she sensed a thread of worry, as if he thought she might call this whole thing off before it got started.

Yeah, right. The building would need to be on fire, *seriously* on fire, for her to stop now. "I want to see you naked." She'd been imagining it since she'd seen him in the towel. Hell, since she'd first laid eyes on him, but now she was sure it was going to happen and she wanted to look her fill. She scooted back on the bed and rested on her elbows, a queen in repose.

He took a step closer, almost on the bed. "That's the goal." His voice had gone gruff, full of sensual promise.

"No. Now." It felt a little wrong to take control like this. She was his boss, sort of. But, if anything, the wrongness made this whole thing ten times hotter.

Was she discovering a new kink? Or was it just Owen?

His eyes lit up when she gave the command. If this was a kink, at least Owen was right there with her. He reached a hand behind his head and pulled off his black t-shirt to reveal that chest that had been driving her crazy. His muscles rippled, and she was almost certain he was flexing, showing off.

Stasia loved it.

His hair was long enough to hang in front of his eyes, having lost the hold of whatever gel he used, and it gave him a playful air. He wasn't a playboy set on seduction. No playboy smiled that openly.

And then his pants came off and Stasia forgot how to breathe.

She'd seen cocks before. She'd had boyfriends. And she was an emergency room doctor. People did weird things with their private parts and she'd seen it all.

But Owen still made her mouth water.

He was plumping up, not completely hard yet but getting close, his thick length nestled in dark hair. She couldn't stop staring. She wanted him inside her. She wanted to taste him. She wanted it all.

Now would be the right time for her to strip. Owen stood before her, fully naked, cock in hand and ready for more, but there was something powerful to laying clothed while her man was fully naked and standing before her. She didn't want to give up the power just yet.

All it took was a crook of her finger to bring him forward.

"Don't I get to see you?" he asked. His eyes looked brighter than brown after a shift of his head moved his hair out of the way. He looked *hungry*, like some kind of predator, and she was his prey, but she was going to bring him to his knees.

"You're looking at me." He was close enough to touch now, and she ran a hand up one of his thighs and over the curve of his spectacular ass.

Owen groaned. "You know that's not what I mean."

Stasia could respond. There was probably some tart reply that would be perfect for the moment.

Instead she licked the length of his cock and then took the head into her mouth, swirling her tongue around and memorizing his taste, earthy, masculine, and *Owen*.

He gasped and nearly fell over in surprise and Stasia took that for a win. Did he still think she was some stuck up princess? She'd show him.

Though there weren't actually any losers in this game.

She couldn't take him fully in without gagging. It

had been a long time since she'd done this, and even if she had the practice, Owen was big. But her hand took care of what her mouth did, sucking him to fullness and luxuriating in the desperate sounds of pleasure he was making.

She could make him come like this. It wouldn't take that much work.

Just the thought of it had her own body shaking with want. She reached down, sneaking one hand into her pants and stroking her slick clit.

She didn't want Owen coming down her throat. She needed him inside of her.

And though it was torture to back up, she let go of him and laid back, leaving the hand in her pants for him to see.

Owen's eyes looked yellow, and there was a pointedness to his face that looked *off*, but Stasia blinked and it was gone. She gasped as she stroked herself, Owen's gaze a hot caress, even if he could only see the outline of her hand.

"You're evil," he said, his own hand back on his cock, but rather than stroking he was holding it tight at the base, too close to coming to do more.

Stasia had to pull her hand out of her pants. "Want me to stop?" There was no chance of stopping. Not now that Owen was there and hard and perfect.

"Never." It was a vow.

"Come here." She pulled him down on top of her and their lips crashed together in a kiss more intimate than sex. If he cared about where her mouth had been a moment ago, he didn't say a word.

Smart man.

She could kiss him all night, and she would have if her body wasn't demanding more. She could kiss Owen later, her body promised, as long as she got him inside of her now.

Yes.

Yes, that sounded very good.

Somehow they managed to get her clothes off and every inch of skin that she had pressed against Owen burned and demanded more. She could become addicted to him. Maybe she already was. Any thoughts of the spark between them fizzling out in the morning were long gone. Now that she'd tasted him, she couldn't give it up. Not now, not ever.

They rolled until Owen was on his back with her laying on top of him, his cock hard between them as they kissed. She got her fingers around him and stroked, swallowing down his moan. She almost crawled right on him then, and it was only the barest edge of sanity that pulled her off.

"Condom?" She might have had some stashed away somewhere, but her mind was too sex crazed to think about it. Owen, though, seemed like the kind of guy that came prepared. Under other circumstances she might give him hell for it, but today she prayed she was right.

"Wallet." The word was guttural, his ability to say much taken away by his hard cock, and it only made her hotter.

Stasia didn't want to pull off. If she was just a bit hornier she might have said damn the consequences and gone through with it. Instead, she scrambled off the bed until she found his pants and wrestled with the pockets until one offered up a leather wallet. And inside she didn't just find *a* condom, she found three.

"Should I be jealous?" There was coming prepared, and then there was this.

"All for you." It should have been cheesy. He was lying in her bed, his cock in hand, looking at her with lust in his yellowy-brown eyes, but it made Stasia's heart beat hard.

She had it bad.

But she wasn't backing down now, not even if the tiniest part of her worried that she was headed for heartbreak.

Getting the condom on his cock was another test of dexterity, but they managed between smiles and kisses.

And then Stasia climbed on, straddling him and guiding his cock to her entrance. He filled her up by inches, further and further until she was certain there was no space left inside of her, and yet, somehow, he still went deeper.

Their eyes locked and an awareness passed between them. For a moment she thought someone else was looking out of Owen's eyes, that flash of yellow she'd been seeing while they made love.

Should it have scared her? She didn't know. It didn't. It felt *right* in the same way all of this encounter felt right.

Meant to be.

She didn't believe in soulmates. She'd never been one for religion. But the thing passing between her and Owen was greater than either one of them and deeper than it had any right to be.

She couldn't call it love, not now, not so soon. But it was much deeper, much truer, than simple lust.

There was nothing simple about this.

She knew deep in her heart that there was no letting Owen go, not now that she had her hooks in him. But figuring out what that meant was going to take work.

The worries washed away as she began to move on top of him, setting the rhythm of their dance. Her body was already taut and teetering at the edge of release, and Owen wouldn't be far behind her.

And then she was rippling around him, crying out his name and babbling nonsense that she was going to pretend she didn't understand. Owen gripped her tight as he came right after her, emptying himself into the condom.

It wasn't over. Not as they separated and he took care of the condom. Not as he lay back down in bed beside her, somehow realizing she wanted a cuddle even if she'd never dare ask for it.

If anything, she wanted him more than she had at the start.

"Stay here tonight." It felt vulnerable to say it. He might have just been buried inside of her, her body still stretched with the memory of him, but some of the hormones had washed away and her defenses were building themselves back up. But were they leaving a door for Owen to slip through?

"Yeah?" He looked thrilled. He wasn't like her. He didn't hide his emotions, he had no secrets. Everything was right there on the surface for anyone to see and it was a kind of bravery Stasia would never possess.

Was this more than a fling to him? Was it possible he was feeling what she was feeling? If she could believe the look on his face, maybe it was real.

But she couldn't just ask. She couldn't be that open. "We've got two more condoms."

He laughed, as if he saw right through her and kissed her.

She was in so much trouble.

CHAPTER FIFTEEN

Stasia didn't mean to let Owen move into her room. It just sort of happened. In the morning he started kissing her and her body was way too sated to kick him out of bed. Plus, he gave really good cuddles, something she'd never really wanted before.

Of course, by the time they came down for breakfast Em had to know what was going on. She grinned at them like they were the funniest pair she'd ever seen, but out of some form of kindness for Stasia's tender nerves, she didn't mention anything.

It was another lazy day around the house. Em was happy for the boredom since her days would be scheduled down to the minute once she was back on tour. Stasia would have been going stir crazy, but Owen and Em managed to keep her entertained.

They watched the sequel to the comedy they'd

watched the night before and Owen sat right next to her again, one arm slung across her shoulders. She didn't even notice at first when she snuggled against him, but by the time she did it was too late to pull away.

And she didn't want to.

And then that night Owen followed her to her room and pulled out a pack of condoms he'd unearthed from her bathroom. It was a bit arrogant, but she loved it. Things just fell into place when it came to him, no matter that the circumstances for their meeting sucked. He felt right and when he kissed her, she saw stars.

If there was any doubt that they were sexually compatible, that went up in flames on the second night. He had her twisted in knots, physically and emotionally, contortions she didn't know were possible. And she still wanted more.

"Do you like being a bodyguard?" she asked when she couldn't fall asleep. She was right next to him, tracing her fingers up and down his abs.

Owen shivered under her touch. "It's a living."

"That's not an answer." She was dealing with her own career crisis and knew just how bad it could be. She didn't want Owen facing the same issues.

"I like being *your* bodyguard." He kissed the side of her neck and nipped her with his teeth, probably leaving a mark she'd be embarrassed of in the morning.

"I bet you say that to all the girls."

She meant it as a joke, but he grew serious. "Just you. This has never happened before."

"Sleeping with a client?" It still sent a zing of the forbidden through her brain, but now that they'd taken the plunge Stasia wasn't going to pull back until she had no other choice.

"Falling for a client." Their eyes met and there was no hint of a joke. He meant every word.

It was way too fast. It normally took Stasia a week to decide if she was even willing to consider going on one date with a guy, and in half that time she'd let Owen into her bed—twice!—and couldn't imagine letting him go.

"Too much?" he asked.

She could reject him now. His eyes would dim and he wouldn't hold her as tight. She could tell him she needed more time or that this was just a fling while they were locked in her house and her brother hunted down the people who meant her harm.

But none of that would be true. She'd just be trying to defend herself from the pain that he could bring her if he ever broke her heart.

"Not too much." She couldn't give him more, she wasn't as open as him, but she wasn't about to push him away. Not now. "Tell me something special about you. You have to have secrets." If her soul felt flayed, she wanted him equally exposed.

He stiffened and a strange look crossed his face.

"You can say you shot a man in Reno just to watch him die if you don't want to tell me." She tried to keep it light, but she'd never been good at jokes, and it came out sourer than she intended.

"I don't want to keep secrets from you," he said. His hand found the nape of her neck and his fingers started to massage it.

"What's the but?"

"It's not only my secret to tell."

"Sounds big." The weight of the world lay all around them, and Stasia regretted summoning it. She'd been lying all happy in the afterglow and then she had to ruin it.

"I promise I'll tell you. Someday."

"Someday." Making promises led to expectations, and Stasia was trying her hardest—and failing—to keep from doing that. She could only guarantee that Owen would be around for a week. Was he really willing to travel all the way from Queens to see her? Dating someone in a different borough was basically a long term relationship in New York terms. And what about his job? What about hers?

"We'll figure it out," Owen said, kissing her hair and reading her mind.

Eventually she slept and dreamt weird dreams that disturbed her but were forgotten by the morning.

She woke alone to cold sheets and vaguely recalled Owen getting out of bed and telling her to keep sleeping. It was near eight o'clock and Stasia felt like she'd slept until noon.

She took her time showering and changing, and before she could head downstairs for some breakfast her phone rang. It was AR.

"What's up?" she asked.

"I have good news." He sounded triumphant, like he'd just managed a coup in a small country.

Stasia's heart sank. There was only one kind of good news he'd be delivering to her. "What is it?"

"We managed to track down the threat against you. Sounds like grabbing you was just stage one of a multi-pronged attack. The perpetrators are being dealt with and you should be safe enough to let the *babysitter* go early." For a second she wondered if AR knew what was going on between her and Owen before she remembered that she was the one who'd originally called Owen a babysitter.

It was Friday. Owen was supposed to be hers until Tuesday.

"Perpetrators? Multiple? You're sure you found everyone? That was quick." She didn't exactly want to suffer another attempted kidnapping, but she was grasping at anything to keep Owen by her side.

"There might be a few stragglers, but the plan is unraveling fast and they won't have the resources to come for you." No doubt her brother was sitting in the middle of the spider web and plucking the strings to close a trap.

"Do you know why they came for me?"

AR sighed. "Objection to a specific project from the company. Details confidential. They planned to hold you hostage until they extracted terms from Selby Group. Not the smartest negotiation tactic."

Because Stasia was worth less than a Selby Group project, probably. She was just the easiest of the Selby children to nab.

"Do you want me to cancel the contract early?" AR asked.

"No. You say there could be stragglers, better safe than sorry. But you can probably call in the surveillance team. No need to keep them tied up." She had almost forgotten about them, and it couldn't be fun to babysit a woman who never left her house.

"I already did. I'm a little surprised about the guard, though."

She didn't want AR to make trouble with Owen's

boss. They'd figure out the road ahead, if there was a road ahead, later.

"He's not as bad as I thought."

"Huh. Well, I have a call. Reach out to my secretary if you change your mind."

He hung up before Stasia could say goodbye. She wasn't going to change her mind. But now she had to figure out how she was going to hold onto Owen for good.

CHAPTER SIXTEEN

Stasia was acting weird and Owen wanted to know why. Ever since she'd come downstairs for breakfast, something had been off. At first he worried that whatever fever of lust and emotion was building between them had been snuffed out, but when Em left them alone for a minute Stasia pushed him up against the wall and kissed him like her life depended on it.

So, no issue with the lust.

"Is staying in the house getting to you?" They'd meandered back to her room at some point and she was sitting in the window seat and looking out at the park. He didn't know what Em was doing, but she seemed happy enough keeping herself entertained in the peace of Stasia's house.

"What?" Stasia looked over at him, but her eyes were far away.

There wasn't much room on the bench for two people, but Owen managed to squeeze in near her feet. "I know it can be frustrating to be stuck inside. We can figure out something if you need a break." It would be difficult. No doubt the surveillance team would hate him, but he'd give Stasia the world if she asked for it.

She blinked hard and gave her head a little shake. "No, it's not that. I really would be a spoiled princess for complaining about being stuck in my house for a few days."

"You're not spoiled." It might have been his first instinct, but that was because he hadn't seen the generosity of her prickly spirit. Stasia didn't warm up to people quickly—Owen was pretty sure he was the exception there—but she gave her all.

She smiled wryly. "I am. A bit. Just not the way you thought."

"When are the servants showing up to wait on us hand and foot then?" Owen wouldn't mind a little pampering, but he couldn't imagine Stasia putting up with it. She had self-sufficient stamped on her forehead.

She reached out, silently asking for his hand, and Owen linked their fingers together. It was a bit awkward and his shoulder didn't like the position, but his heart loved it. Any reason to touch Stasia.

Mate.

His wolf needed to learn to shut the hell up. It was still restless under his skin; the only moments where they felt like one came when he was buried deep in Stasia, her scent covering him. He wondered if a run would fix it, but it was risky to run in the city, not that anyone would actually believe he was a wolf if they saw him.

Could he tell Stasia about that part of himself? Would she believe him?

Seeing was believing.

But he couldn't just shift right there and show her. She was liable to kick him out of her house and her life for good. No one knew werewolves existed, at least not anyone that Owen knew who wasn't already a werewolf. And the team probably wouldn't take too kindly to him spilling the secrets four days into knowing someone.

It might have only been four days, but his heart didn't care.

And his wolf knew what she was, even if his mind was still struggling to keep up.

"They—" Stasia began to speak but his phone rang. Owen would have let it ring, but she said, "Take it. Don't let me stop you."

He read the caller ID and had to leave the room. Andre was calling, and there was no way he'd reach out if it wasn't important. "What's up?" Owen asked.

He heard heavy breathing and a muffled command to *speed up, goddamnit* before Andre spoke. "Vega got shot. It's—fuck! Take the back roads, it's faster." Andre cursed more before talking to Owen again. "The wound isn't closing."

Owen's own mind threw out some choice curses, and his wolf growled at the thought of his packmate in danger. He wasn't exactly close to Vega, but the man was family. "What happened? How?" One of the perks they'd discovered about their wolfishness was crazy fast healing. A knife wound that would have needed hundreds of stitches could heal in an hour. A gunshot went from fatal to barely bruised just as quickly.

"Job was ending. Gibson and I were there for wrap up. Things went bad. Cops showed up and we piled him into the car. Had to leave Gibson behind to deal with it. Willa, hurry!" It was bad if Andre was using anyone's first name, especially Willa's.

"Why's he still hurt?" Owen paced and tried to think of a way to fix it. They didn't have a doctor, though they all had some basic medic training. It hadn't seemed necessary when they thought they were basically invincible.

"I. Don't. Know." The words were practically growled. "He needs a doctor."

"You can't take him to a hospital." He hated even saying it, but their secret couldn't come out. Owen didn't know if anything wolfy would show up in blood tests, but they couldn't risk it. The military had discharged them all before the first change hit, but he feared they'd pull them all back if they got a hint of the truth.

"I know that." Andre took even breaths. "You need to bring the doc to the safe house."

"The doc?" It didn't hit at first, and when it did, Owen's wolf went wild. "What? No! She's not a part of this."

"Bryan is going to die if he doesn't see a doctor," Andre hissed, as if he didn't want Willa or Vega to hear. "We need her. There's no other choice."

There had to be. Owen wracked his brain, hoping to latch onto one. But he had a highly skilled ER doctor sitting in the next room who was his best hope at saving his friend's life.

She'd never forgive him if she found out he didn't give her a chance to try.

"Keep him alive until we get there." Owen disengaged the call and took a deep breath before marching back into Stasia's bedroom.

She must have read something on his face.

"What's wrong?" She got up off the bench and came to him.

Owen couldn't be her lover now, not when time was so short. "One of my co-workers needs medical attention. We can't take him to the hospital. Do you have supplies?"

They had a pretty extensive first aid kit at the safe house, but he hoped Stasia had more.

"What kind of attention? If it's bad enough to need a hospital, that's where he should be." Her forehead creased in worry even as she moved to her dresser and started pulling out clothes.

"I know it doesn't make sense, but he can't go to the hospital. It's not safe." What was he supposed to say? Sorry, babe, your bodyguard is a werewolf and so are all of his friends?

Her head snapped up. "You're not… this isn't something illegal, is it?"

"No. I promise." He didn't know about any laws against werewolves.

She gave him a hard look for several seconds. Owen felt every one of them tick by, knowing that was another drop of blood spilling out of Bryan Vega. But whatever she saw did the trick. She gave him a nod.

"There's a kit in the library. Grab it. Tell Em we're going. We'll take your car."

"I'll call the surveillance team." He didn't know what to tell them, and he certainly didn't want them following to the farm, but he'd figure something out.

Strangely, Stasia winced. "I was going to tell you. AR called them off. Apparently the threat's been handled."

Owen was missing something there. Something important. But his thoughts were in a whirl, too focused on Vega's predicament to get a handle on it. For the moment he was just thankful for the good fortune. "I'll get your bag."

They had to hurry. Vega didn't have much time.

CHAPTER SEVENTEEN

THIS WAS wrong in about a thousand ways and Stasia could lose her medical license. But given the way that Owen was swerving through the streets and cutting through New York traffic like they were in a live action video game, it had to be serious. A man's life was in danger. She was the only one that could help.

In the back seat, Em cursed. She'd piled in the car right behind them, and though Owen had glared, he hadn't wasted time arguing with her about coming. It was that serious.

But why couldn't his co-worker go to the hospital? Was there a citizenship issue? An arrest warrant? Something else? Owen promised it wasn't illegal, but she couldn't think of a non-shady reason for someone to avoid the hospital for a life-threatening issue.

They crossed over into Brooklyn and weaved through the streets until Owen pulled up in front of a warehouse. Stasia clutched her supply bag tight. This place wasn't going to be sterile, and infection was a threat she'd be fighting to the end.

"Come on." Owen parked the car and led them through the door. It wasn't as bad inside as she feared; the building was set up with offices and it was brightly lit, almost pleasant. Or it would have been if she didn't hear someone moaning in pain.

They started to run.

Stasia burst through the door to one of the rooms and found a man lying on an exam table with another man holding him down and a woman holding a bloodied rag over his shoulder.

The muscle could be fucked, but he was alive so his heart probably wasn't hit.

She didn't waste time wondering why this office/warehouse had a medical exam room in it, nor did she bother with introductions. She went to the sink on the side of the room and washed her hands as best she could.

"Wash your hands," she told Owen and Em, "I may need you." She didn't know about the other two people, but from the way her patient was squirming, they were trying to keep him from moving too much. The damage may have already been done.

"What happened?" Stasia demanded of the woman applying pressure.

She looked up and she couldn't have been more than twenty-five, bright blue eyes full of fear and confusion. Then she blinked and snapped out of it. "Gunshot. Right shoulder. Handgun, possibly nine millimeter. Bryan's been shot before, why isn't it closing up?" she demanded.

"Willa!" snapped the man holding her patient down.

"She needs to know, Andre."

Willa. Andre. Bryan. Stasia filed those names away. "Any exit wound?" She didn't know what Willa meant about the wound closing, probably just panic, even though she'd given the report with poise. They didn't have time to worry. The t-shirt she was holding against the wound was soaked and, as far as she knew, she didn't have any blood to transfuse.

"No," said Willa.

"Okay." This was going to be quick and dirty. Stasia had a scalpel with her and she needed to see what she could do. Digging the bullet out would likely cause more harm than good, but she had to get her eyes on it, see what the situation was.

She approached her patient. Bryan was moving, but his eyes were closed and he didn't seem aware of what was going on. "Bryan, can you hear me?" she asked.

He moaned in pain.

"Bryan," she tried again, "I'm going to help you. This may hurt." It would. No way around that. She wasn't in the habit of carrying around strong drugs, but they'd worry about the shock of pain later.

Bryan kept moaning.

No more time to waste. She met Willa's eyes. "Was there any blood spurting when you began applying pressure?"

"No, just regular bleeding."

"Good. I need you to remove that t-shirt and go to his feet. Hold them down. He's probably going to move when I start cutting." She hated to think it. Even on the darkest days in Bermeja she hadn't needed to cut into semi-conscious patients.

Willa moved. Stasia could feel Em and Owen standing behind her, but she ignored them. This was her element and she had to do her thing.

She met Andre's eyes. "You ready?"

He nodded.

She assessed the wound and scowled at the way his skin had gone an almost impossible gray color, as if some of the dye from the shirt had soaked into it. She hoped that was it; she had no idea what could cause the issue otherwise.

She wasn't a surgeon, but she had general training and she could do this.

Stasia sliced deeper into her patient's wound and revealed the torn muscle underneath. "Give me light," she demanded, and a few seconds later a flashlight shined over her shoulder. It must have been either Owen or Em, but she didn't look back to check.

It didn't take long to find the bullet. It wasn't lodged deep and she was distantly curious as to why it was causing her patient so much trouble. Sure, it should have hurt like a motherfucker, but it wasn't near anything vital and it wasn't that deep.

"Forceps," she demanded.

"What?" asked Em, who she could hear rooting around in her bag.

"The giant tweezers. And I'll need the suture kit next."

"Got it." They were shoved into Stasia's hand.

She carefully extracted the piece of metal from the wound and dropped it into a container that Owen was holding. She only looked away for a second, but when she examined the wound again, it was smaller.

Impossibly smaller.

Her patient's eyes snapped open and he let out a bellowing roar.

"Hold him!" Stasia demanded of Andre and Willa. The bullet was out, but he was far from safe.

But Bryan was a man possessed and he struggled against them. The forceps went flying out of her hand as he surged up, and then the scalpel fell too, catching her forearm along the way with a bright, stinging stripe of red.

His eyes were wide and shifted from blue to yellow as something began to happen to his face. Stasia didn't understand it. She couldn't figure it out. This wasn't medical. It wasn't possible. He shouldn't have that much energy to begin with, let alone be... changing.

Fur started to spring up and his bones slid around with gross cracks. It couldn't have taken more than a few seconds and Stasia was rooted in place in fascination and fear.

Someone put a hand on her shoulder, as if trying to pull her back. She could distantly hear someone saying something, but the roaring of the beast in front of her drowned it all out.

Werewolf.

It should have been shocking. Should have been impossible. But she was seeing it with her own two eyes. What was there to disbelieve? Her hands had just been in this man's flesh. There was no way this was a trick.

The change took her patient and he was suddenly a huge wolf. Andre tried to grab for him and Willa must have fallen back, but nothing stopped the wolf from launching himself straight at her and digging his teeth into her shoulder.

Stasia screamed.

CHAPTER EIGHTEEN

OWEN WAS CAUGHT between the need to protect Stasia and the need to rip Bryan Vega's throat out for daring to come near his mate. His wolf roared to the surface and demanded he shift, but he fought the change. He'd be no help to anyone on paws.

He got between Em and Bryan and pushed the woman back before rearing forward and grabbing Vega by the scruff of his neck and pulling him off of Stasia. Stasia showed more presence of mind than expected and kicked out with one foot until the wolf stumbled back.

Andre took over then, leaping at Vega and tackling him to the floor.

It all happened in a handful of seconds.

"What's going on in here?" Gibson burst into the

room, Rowe and Jackson right behind him, and took in the scene: Stasia clutching her shoulder, Em backed in a corner, and Andre holding a shifted Vega to the ground while Willa stood frozen at the foot of the exam table.

"Stasia!" Em got a good look at her sister and charged forward, not paying any attention to the werewolf on the ground or the army major in the doorway.

Owen's wolf bristled at the thought of anyone getting close to his mate, but he could reason with the beast. Em was her sister; she wouldn't do anything to harm their mate. She could be trusted. Still, he let out a little growl and took a step closer.

He didn't want anyone else near Stasia.

"I'm fine," Stasia was saying. "This needs to be cleaned. Probably stitched too. And I think there's a wound on my arm." She didn't sound like a woman who had just discovered werewolves existed, but he had a feeling she was relying on her training. She had to take care of her problems before she could even think about breaking down.

Owen wanted to turn around and care for Stasia, but he had to protect her from any threats, and right now *everything* was a potential threat. He distantly knew that the others in the room were people he should be able to trust, but Vega had bit Stasia. Anyone could do her more harm.

"What's going on here?" Gibson repeated, and from his tone he wasn't going to ask a third time.

Vega made a sad sound, and Andre let him up once it was clear the wolf wasn't about to fly off into a rage.

Owen growled. Vega needed to pay for what he'd done, but Willa put herself between him and Vega, stopping the fight from happening before it could start. Owen might have been grateful for that at another time, but now he just wanted to attack Willa too.

"Dr. Nichols extracted something from Vega's shoulder," said Willa, finally answering Gibson's question when no one else would. "He immediately started to shift and he attacked her. I don't think he knew what was going on."

"Take Vega out of here. Watch him. You too, Jackson," Gibson demanded. His face was dark with anger and Owen knew the blow up wouldn't be good.

Willa, Jackson, and Vega left, which still left the rest of the pack. It should have been a happy family, but his mate was bleeding and she needed help.

Gibson looked over his shoulder to Stasia. "We're—"

She cut him off. "Tell me about werewolves later. One of you has to have some medic training. I need stitches. Unless you're willing to take *me* to a hospital?" He didn't look back at her, but he could imagine the challenge in his mate's eyes and pride suffused him. Not many people could stand up to Gibson, but Stasia did it without a thought.

"Rowe." Gibson didn't need to say more. Rowe had the most medic training out of all of them and definitely knew how to clean a wound and give stitches.

Owen stopped him.

"Move aside," Leland Rowe said quietly.

"No." He was fighting his wolf with all he had to keep from lashing out. He needed to keep Stasia safe and his wolf was certain that letting anyone near her would be a mistake. And given how the past hour had gone, he couldn't disagree.

"Owen! He needs to look." Stasia sounded out of breath, and that was finally enough for him to move. She was pale—even paler than usual—and sweat beaded on her forehead. Em was holding gauze to her wound, but it was already starting to bleed through.

And still his wolf wouldn't move. They needed to protect their mate.

"Gordon," said Gibson. And Owen didn't know

why, but a second later Andre barreled into him and charged until they were both out of the room. Gibson slammed the door and Owen heard him throw the lock.

He howled and fought against Andre's grip.

"I need to be in there. She needs me." His teeth were longer than they should have been and his vision was *off* in the way it sometimes got when he shifted to his other form. He was losing control of his human form as his wolf demanded to take over.

Owen wanted to surrender to it; he wanted to take the power his wolf could give him and prevent anyone from touching Stasia ever again.

"Calm down before I cuff you," Andre threatened.

Not much could hold an enraged werewolf, but Gibson had found some old fashioned manacles that could do the trick. Owen had wondered why he thought he needed them, but the threat was enough to make him think that maybe Gibson had a point. And he knew Andre would tie him up without hesitation.

"I'm calm," Owen promised, even though his heart was pounding so hard he could hear it in his ears.

"You're not." Andre glared at him, but he did loosen his grip. "Come on. I don't know what's going on, but you probably should get a little distance."

"Try and move me." Owen was out of the room. He couldn't see his mate, but the scent of her blood still tickled his senses. "I can't stop Rowe from touching her, but I'm not moving another foot."

CHAPTER NINETEEN

Leland Rowe had kind eyes and a steady hand, but that didn't make the stitches any less painful. Em was right beside her, gripping her uninjured arm in support while Rowe worked on her shoulder.

But Stasia wanted Owen.

She had to shove the thought as far back in her mind as she could. Owen had freaked out royally even though *she* was the one who'd been unknowingly operating on a freaking werewolf. If she was being reasonable, she'd probably agree with Owen's assessment that they couldn't take Vega to a hospital.

Instead she wanted to yell. But if she yelled and flailed as much as she wanted, she was going to rip out the stitches that Rowe had already done and ruin whatever he had left to do.

"You're not too bad at that," she said. She wanted to ask if he was a werewolf too. Were they all?

Was *Owen*?

Or were they all just keeping Vega's secret.

Which was worse?

"Medic field training," Rowe responded.

"Army?" asked Em after giving Stasia's fingers a squeeze. She had to be freaking out nearly as much as Stasia, but she seemed calm enough for now.

"Yes." Rowe finished off the stitch and bandaged the wound, which was right at the bend of her shoulder and was bound to hurt every time Stasia shifted.

She twisted her arm and winced at the pull of the stitches, but she had to see the damage the scalpel had done to her forearm. Except there wasn't a wound there. The skin was unblemished.

How?

She remembered the stinging pain as the blade sliced her and there was blood on her shirt from where she'd pressed her arm tight against it to stem the flow. But now it looked like nothing had happened. Had she been mistaken? It was easy to get confused when an angry werewolf was lunging at you.

It had to be that. Stasia poked at her arm to make

sure the wound wasn't somehow hiding, but that didn't do anything.

"Something wrong?" Em asked quietly as Rowe backed away.

"I thought..." Stasia didn't want to say, afraid it would make her sound crazy, as if anything could sound crazy after what just happened. "I'm fine."

Em scoffed. "You just got bit by a fucking werewolf." She shuddered and her expression slipped, but she pasted on her best smile, the kind she flashed at audiences every night on tour. Em could pretend everything was okay and Stasia was going to follow her example.

Rowe stood next to Gibson and they were both looking at her like she was about to grow a second head... or fur. She wanted Owen there. Em could hold her hand like a champ, but there was something about Owen's presence that made her feel safe. Protected.

Loved.

It was too soon for that. She could barely stand to think it. And pretty soon her mind was going to catch up to this whole situation and she was going to be pissed as fuck at Owen and the rest of them. He *knew* what Vega was. He'd put her at risk.

Oh. Well, there was the anger. It burned away the

pain of the stitches and Stasia stood up from where she'd been sitting.

The door opened behind Gibson and Owen came rushing back in. He didn't stop until he was right in front of her, those soulful eyes of his roving over her, making sure she was alright. He snagged on the stitches on her shoulder where her shirt had been ripped away, and she swore she heard him growl.

Werewolf?

Man?

"What's going on, Owen?" She wanted to throw herself in his arms and demand that he make everything okay. He was her bodyguard, even if the main threat was taken care of. But that didn't matter. She didn't want him to leave *ever*, even if she was mad at him.

"Let's take this somewhere a little less bloody," Gibson said, interrupting their reunion.

Owen did reach out and touch her then, careful to avoid the stitches, and holding her like she was precious. After a second he laced their fingers together and led her out of the room to wherever Gibson was taking them. Em followed closely behind.

The new location turned out to be something like a large break room with a few couches and chairs and a huge TV hanging on one wall.

"This is a nice place," said Em with a bit of surprise as she sank down onto one of the plush chairs.

Stasia wanted to stand, but between the rush of treating Vega and the adrenaline from the bite, she was about to crash. She sank down onto the nearest couch and didn't complain when Owen sat next to her.

It only took another few minutes for the rest of the team—pack?—to join them. Andre Gordon, Willa Hunter, Leland Rowe, Erin Jackson, and even Bryan Vega, who had managed to shift back to his human form and only had a bit of bruised and reddened skin on his naked shoulder to show for the bullet wound.

"Am I going to turn into a werewolf?" Stasia's heart was beating madly, but she sounded cool. She wasn't exactly sure how she was dealing, but unless she started screaming she was going to hold to the equilibrium as long as she could. She looked directly at Owen and asked again. "Am I?"

His mouth opened and closed a few times and his eyes widened.

"We don't know." It was Gibson who answered. "No one's ever bit another person before." He glared at Vega.

The young man—and he was young, at least ten years younger than Stasia—hung his head and let out a shuddering breath before he looked up again and met her eyes. "I'm sorry. So sorry."

Maybe Stasia was supposed to forgive him, but how could she? She just nodded and that seemed to satisfy the kid. Good. She didn't have any more to give.

"Are you *all* werewolves?" Owen's heat was enough to burn, and maybe she should have pulled away from him if he was secretly a monster, but nothing about him made her think he was monstrous, even if he was a werewolf.

"We are," Gibson confirmed.

"Were you born that way?" Em asked.

Good question. She was so glad that Em had jumped in the car with them. She was going to need moral support soon, or at least Em's memory. Trauma had a way of messing with a person's head.

"No," said Gibson.

"Then shouldn't you know about the bite?" It *hurt*, and Stasia didn't want bullshit answers. She'd done a good deed, she'd saved a fucking life. She deserved to know the truth. Her boyfriend/bodyguard was apparently a werewolf, and he hadn't bothered to say a word about that. She'd been bitten by a freaking werewolf. And now they were playing word games. "Tell me what's going on."

There was a heavy silence in the room after

Stasia's demand. She was worried no one would speak, but finally Owen broke the silence.

"It started two years ago in Germany."

CHAPTER TWENTY

Two years ago

The last thing Owen remembered, he was going off the base. He wasn't sure why. But that was normal enough. He sure as hell hadn't meant to end up in the middle of a forest somewhere, his hands tied and in the middle of some strange ritual put on by devil worshipers.

Were they devil worshipers? Did devil worshipers actually exist?

He remembered hearing about them when he was a kid and he had thought it was all fake. But now he was in the middle of some magic looking circle and there was a guy wearing a black robe with animal pelts over his shoulders and they were surrounded by guards carrying wicked looking guns.

Would devil worshipers need guns?

His mind felt kind of spacey and his head ached. Had he been hit? That was very possible. He wanted to feel around for a wound, but with his hands tied he could barely move. And the tactical part in the back of his mind told him it would be a bad idea for the warlock in the middle of the circle to figure out that he was awake.

Warlock? Witch? Sorcerer? It was way too *Lord of the Rings* for him.

But whoever the magic man was, he wasn't paying attention to Owen right then, so Owen did his best to look around without squirming too much. And he wasn't the only person tied up.

He wasn't sure of the others' names, though he was pretty sure the older guy was a freaking major. In fact, he thought he recognized everyone from the base. Abducting a handful of US soldiers off of an army base couldn't be easy, and it was pretty fucking suicidal. Did they think the Army was going to play? They would come in guns blazing to get their people back.

And this was Germany. It was supposed be safe. He had been psyched to get this assignment. Ending up tied up in the woods like he was playing a part in an old-fashioned fairytale was not how Owen expected things to go.

There were seven torches blazing all around them and the warlock was doing something on an altar in the middle of them. Was this human sacrifice? Owen's mom was going to freak out if she found out he was killed by human sacrifice. She was a good Catholic woman and no priest would be able to explain this.

The warlock turned to him, carrying a scary, shiny knife.

"You don't have to do this." This was the time to reason with him, if it was possible to reason with some kind of demon summoner out of one of Grimm's fairy tales.

The man didn't speak, his lips pulled into a terrifying smile with two sharp teeth. They didn't look human. Was he human? Maybe he was a demon.

"No, no, no!" Owen tried to struggle, but the man didn't pause. And he brought the knife down, but he didn't stab him. Instead he sliced a healthy stripe of skin on his chest, enough to sting and draw blood, but not enough to do much damage.

What the fuck? Then he caught some of the dripping blood in a metal cup of some kind. No, a chalice. That was the right name for a fancy magic cup.

The warlock or demon continued the ritual with

each of the tied up soldiers. One of the guards stepped into the light and Owen got a good look at his face. He did his best to memorize it. If he got out of this thing, he wanted to come for these people. He wanted them to pay for whatever weird shit they were doing.

But the warlock was done with whatever strange task he was performing and he went back to the center of the circle.

He started to chant. Owen didn't have any special skill in languages, but he could recognize a few from being stationed around the world. This wasn't one he recognized. It didn't sound like anything that came from Earth. It was deep and guttural and it made his ears hurt.

The skin where he had been cut started to burn as the man kept chanting, and Owen had to be going crazy because it was like a light show started in front of his eyes. First it was blue light swirling around in circles, and he wondered if it was some kind of LED set up. But there was nothing technological out here. And then a red light joined it and the two lights danced in the air and circled like a cyclone.

The warlock's voice got louder and louder, and Owen was sure that his ears were starting to bleed. He lost sight of the guards, and it was as if they had drifted away into the dark of the forest to give the warlock privacy for this part of his ritual.

The warlock gave a cry and the blue and red lights burst up in a tower of energy before swooping down again and attacking Owen and his fellow prisoners.

He could feel the power with the force of a punch that knocked all of the air out of him.

He breathed in, but his lungs were on fire and the pain grew more and more until he couldn't take it anymore and he passed out.

He woke up, but he was sure he was dead.

Was this heaven?

Maybe not. He hoped not. The US Army owned his body, but he had never signed away his soul. And he recognized the uniforms all around them. It was a smaller squad than he would have expected. They were checking with him and his fellow prisoners, and there was a medic there to give them oxygen and make sure they stayed alive.

Looking around, it didn't look like anything had happened. There was no altar. No torches. No warlock. Owen's bindings had been released and he reached up to touch the cut on his chest, but it was gone.

A hallucination?

He didn't have that strong of an imagination.

Things had proceeded very fast after that and Owen barely had time to think.

He had years left on his contract, but politics had a way of screwing up anyone's career, and before long, Owen found himself discharged with healthy severance and orders to keep quiet about the whole thing.

The Army didn't want it getting out that soldiers had been abducted off of one of their bases. And if they had any idea about what had been done to them, they weren't saying.

That was when Owen got to know Major Gibson. The man came to him first as they were debriefing in the States and suggested that maybe it would be a good idea for them to stick together.

Yeah. They were the only people who understood what had really happened. Sticking together seemed like a good idea.

***

ONE YEAR and nine months ago

It wasn't the full moon. It was night and the moon was big, but it wasn't full.

In the past three months, they had begun to put

together a private protection company. Gibson had contacts and he was putting out feelers.

But they were spending a lot of time on his farm in Pennsylvania. And that night they were all outside in the chilly air sitting around a fire and roasting marshmallows.

Hunter felt it first. She stiffened where she sat, putting the stick she was using to char her marshmallow down.

"You okay?" asked Jackson. She reached out a hand to squeeze Hunter's shoulder.

"I—" Hunter collapsed off the small bench she was sitting on and they all sprang into motion.

But what happened next was even stranger than the night in the German forest. Hunter screamed and pulled at all of her clothes until they sat in a heap next to her, and then her body started to shift, fur growing where it definitely shouldn't grow, face elongating until she had a snout, and teeth getting long and deadly.

She shifted to a wolf and howled.

And that howl was what it took for the change to rip through the rest of them.

Owen had no idea how long it took. It didn't hurt. Not that much. And once his body shifted from man to wolf, he didn't care about how it was impossible.

All he wanted to do was run.

And so they ran together, their first time as a pack.

And hours later, when they shifted back, none of them worse for wear, they huddled together and realized that whatever had been done to them in Germany was serious.

PRESENT DAY

Owen looked down at Stasia and tried to read her face. He hated that he could still see the bandage from the stitched up bite on her shoulder. He could kill Vega for attacking her. It didn't matter that it wasn't the young man's fault. This was Owen's mate. He would die to protect her.

"I wish we could tell you more," he said. "But we've been figuring out this whole werewolf thing on our own. None of us were bitten. We don't know if that's real or not. And we don't know what's going to happen to you. But we, *I*, will protect you."

Stasia took a deep breath and nodded. Owen leaned forward and kissed her forehead. He wanted to do more than that. He wanted to hide her away from the rest of this group until they had more information about what was going to happen. But he had a feeling she wasn't going to allow herself to be hidden away.

Her face was completely blank, and then she blinked and gave him a brave smile. "So I might be turning into a werewolf. Great. Does anyone have snacks?"

CHAPTER TWENTY-ONE

Stasia wasn't sure how much longer she could put on a brave face. Werewolves. Freaking werewolves. Her shoulder twinged in response to the bite she was trying hard not to think about, and she couldn't help but wonder if she would be howling at the moon soon enough.

She and Em escaped to the exam room to take a few minutes for themselves now that they had the story from Owen. Everyone else had agreed with his retelling, so she figured it wasn't too far off from the truth.

A warlock had turned them into werewolves in some sort of magic ritual in the Black Forest in Germany. She knew a fairytale when she heard one, but considering she had seen a man turn into a wolf with her own two eyes, she believed it. It didn't matter that her medically-trained brain was protesting that it was impossible. She'd seen it and there was no way it was a trick.

She sank down into one of the chairs in the exam room as Em leaned against the counter. Stasia couldn't stand for another minute. Her legs were shaky and she felt perched on the edge of a panic attack. It was only her sister's presence that was keeping her sane at the moment.

"How are you holding up? Em asked. She reached for something on the counter, the small container into which Stasia had dumped the bullet that had hit Vega, and started switching it from hand to hand, fidgeting. It was an old habit of hers, one she only fell back on when she was nervous.

The container wasn't a toy and it certainly wasn't sanitary, but Stasia couldn't think about that right now.

"I really don't know." She had seen weird things before. That came with the kind of upbringing she had and the job she'd gone into. Plenty of weird shit ended up in the ER. But she had never imagined werewolves.

How was she supposed to react? Was she supposed to get mad at Owen for lying to her? *Could* she? When would that conversation have even come up? Before they fucked? It wasn't like he thought lycanthropy was a sexually transmitted disease. And there was no way she would have believed him anyway.

"It's kind of cool, right?" Em didn't sound so sure as she spoke, but there was a bit of childish wonder underlying her tone.

"Cool?" That was one word. Though Stasia's childhood obsessions had run more towards vampires than werewolves. But it was one thing to fantasize about the otherworldly and something completely different to find out it was real.

"I mean, yeah. Your boyfriend is like a superhero or something." She set the container down and picked up one of the tools lying on the counter and poked at the bullet.

Was he her boyfriend? Stasia didn't deny it, even if they probably needed to have a talk. More than one. "What are you doing?" She pushed out of the chair and came to stand close to Em to see what she was looking at. And she was relieved when her sister didn't back away. It hadn't even occurred to Stasia to fear that, but now she realized her sister might be afraid. "You're not freaked out I might turn into a monster, are you?"

Em laughed. "I've seen you PMSing. I know exactly how much of a monster you can be." She picked up the bullet with a clean set of forceps and inspected it. "Do you have something to wash this off?"

"Why?" Stasia asked as she found what her sister needed. Em had always had an inquisitive mind and she probably would have been an investigator of some kind if she hadn't become a popstar.

"They were freaked out about it. I'm going to assume that they don't normally deal with this kind of thing. And if the legends are anything to go by, shouldn't they have a super healing factor or something? This was a *tiny* little bullet. Even a human could have shaken that off." She put the container down on the table and took a package of saline that Stasia found sitting on the counter. She washed off the blood to reveal the spent bullet.

It looked like a bullet. But Stasia wasn't sure it was *just* a bullet. She hadn't dealt with many gunshot wounds. And those that she had, she hadn't finished the bullet out. It often caused more damage to even try.

"There's something extra on here," Em said as she picked up the washed off bullet with the forceps and brought it close to her face.

"What do you mean?" How could there be something extra on a bullet?

"Look." Em shook the forceps a little as if that

would give Stasia a clue. "It almost looks like it fused with something."

"You're looking at the bullet?" They both jumped as Rowe interrupted them. He was standing in the open doorway and watching them curiously.

It wasn't like they had anything to hide, even if Stasia felt like maybe they should. "We're working on the assumption that you guys heal faster than normal people," she said. "Would I be right about that?" Given the way Vega healed the second the bullet was out of him, it had to be true.

Rowe nodded and came fully into the room. "We've had some reckless play, trying to figure out our limits. It takes a lot of damage to keep us down."

"So not just one bullet?" asked Em.

"That would be correct."

"What about a silver bullet?" she asked, waving the forceps with more trust than Stasia had in them. "Or a bullet with silver stuff on it."

"What?" That got Rowe all the way across the room to look closer at the bullet. "You think someone shot a silver bullet at us?"

Em shrugged. "Or maybe it hit something silver before it hit Vega?" she suggested. "Maybe a fork or a candlestick?"

Rowe thought for a moment as he looked at the tiny piece of metal that had almost killed his friend.

"There were silver candlesticks around us, so it's possible the bullet went through one and fused with the silver." He took the forceps from Em and got a better look at the bullet.

He dropped it onto his hand and flinched as it touched his skin, then he curled his fingers around it and held tight for about five seconds before tossing it back into the container. When he opened his hand back up, there was a red welt that kind of looked like a mosquito bite.

"I was expecting something a little bit more dramatic," Stasia admitted. Going by the movies his skin should have been ghastly, not just minorly irritated. Of course, she wasn't living in a movie.

Row gave a little laugh. "Me too, honestly. That's why I flinched. We've played with silver. How could we not? We're freaking werewolves. But it's really hard to find silver weaponry and it's kind of soft metal. But maybe someone figured something out. I have to tell this to Gibson." Rowe picked up the container with the bullet in it.

"Of course." Stasia probably would have told the boss herself if she'd had a few more minutes to think about it. "This is the first major medical issue you've had, isn't it?" Stasia asked. It hurt her to think that it could have been Owen lying on that table. She didn't know the rest of them very well but they seemed nice enough. Now she understood why they couldn't go to a hospital.

Rowe nodded. "It's mostly been cuts and bruises," he said. "I have enough medic training to handle that. And we heal fast enough that I usually don't need to. There was a bout of food poisoning, too. But again, we get better."

"You have. So far. But what if I hadn't gotten that bullet out of Vega?" She didn't know if the bullet could have killed him. She didn't know *anything*. But already her doctor brain was working hard to think about the things that this pack needed. And an actual trained physician could do them a lot of good.

"Maybe you should talk to Gibson about that," Rowe suggested. "I'm going to go talk to him about the bullet now. Do you two need anything?"

They didn't. Rowe left them alone and Stasia sat back down. Maybe it was time to think about how to put her skills to use in a new field.

CHAPTER TWENTY-TWO

OWEN WAS ready to tear the office apart looking for Stasia. First he demanded that Rowe tell him where she was, but Rowe didn't know. Em was by herself in the kitchen, and no one else had answers.

Owen's wolf threatened to take over and use his superior senses to hunt her down, but he wasn't about to do that. Not right now. He had a feeling that Stasia had enough of wolves for one day and she wouldn't be eager to see him in his other form.

That did not make his wolf happy. But he didn't have time to soothe the beast. Later. He just had to find Stasia and then everything would be alright.

She wasn't in the bedrooms upstairs. Gibson had insisted on building the sleeping quarters just in case they needed to house a client or crash in the city, and today it finally made sense.

Finally he checked the warehouse. They didn't use it for much, though it did make a good training area with all that open space. He found her sitting on a stack of pallets, her legs swinging back and forth, and the pallets rocking precariously with each movement. But Stasia didn't seem too concerned about falling over. She gave him a wan smile when she saw him.

Owen walked up to her, but he made himself leave some distance between them. He wanted to gather her up in his arms, wanted to hold her close, and kiss her, and claim her, and fuck her until they both forgot their names. His wolf knew it was the right thing to do. The man wasn't so sure.

"Enjoying the scenery?" he asked. He wanted to ask her if she was okay, but he had a feeling she might scream if he did. They were all concerned about her well-being. And if she was sitting in an empty warehouse rather than in any of the furnished rooms, he had a feeling she was trying to escape that concern.

"This is really the best New York has to offer, isn't it?" Her tone was wry, but she gave him a little smile.

She was joking. That was good. She didn't joke that often, and certainly not when things were incredibly serious.

"I don't know. There's a dumpster out back that

the tourists can't get enough of." He couldn't resist taking one step closer, but he didn't touch her. If he touched her he didn't think he was going to stop.

"I'm fine," she said, but it sounded like she was trying to convince herself. "I can see that you want to ask. The shoulder doesn't really hurt that much. I took a couple ibuprofen and that seems to have helped. I don't seem to be growing any weird fur. And I don't feel the need to chase squirrels." She shifted on the pallet, but the pallets shifted under her in return so she hopped off of them to keep from falling.

"That's not why I came out here," Owen said. She was so close that he could nuzzle against her. Would she stop him? He was practically vibrating with the need to close the distance between them, but he tried his best to hold still.

"Then why did you? Obviously you're all concerned that I'm about to turn into a werewolf." She shook her head in disbelief. "How is this my life?"

"I should have told you." He didn't know how she wasn't steaming mad at him right now. It was the biggest secret he had to keep, and it had never occurred to him to even mention it to her. Only when he was driving her to come look at Vega had he wondered if he should say something. But they didn't talk about it to outsiders.

But Stasia wasn't an outsider.

"If you had told me, I wouldn't have believed you. I would have thought you were crazy. But I guess I understand why you couldn't take Vega to the hospital."

"I'm still sorry."

"Okay. So why *did* you come out here?"

"I just wanted to be by you." He wasn't one to hide his emotions. He felt what he felt and wasn't ashamed of it. He never wanted to leave Stasia's side, and the hour or so that they had spent apart today was more than enough. Did that make him clingy? He hoped not. It was all too new between them for him to want to walk away yet.

"Is something wrong?" she asked, face scrunched up as if she were trying to solve the problem.

He wasn't hiding the driving need inside of him well enough. "I want to kiss you." They hadn't kissed in hours and he was starving for it.

"That doesn't sound like a problem."

"If I kiss you, I don't know if I could stop." The honesty was raw, ripped right out of his chest and leaving his soul there for her.

"That doesn't sound like a problem," she repeated.

Owen didn't need to be told twice. He closed the

distance between them and wrapped his arms around her, bringing their mouths together in a passionate kiss. Her body fit against him like it was made for him and he would never get enough of the silky soft feel of her skin.

She opened her mouth under his and let his tongue plunder her. Her taste surrounded him and Owen groaned. This was perfect. This was pleasure.

This wasn't enough. He hiked one of her legs up and then the other, urging her to wrap her legs around his waist and give him all of her weight. And then he backed her up until she was resting on that precarious pile of pallets and gave everything over to the kiss.

His cock was iron hard and trapped between them, and he would trade everything he owned for the power to magically incinerate their clothes so he could fuck her right there.

But he heard a car honk outside, and it was a grim reminder that anyone could walk in at any time.

This was something private, something between him and Stasia. He wasn't going to let anyone else see them.

A service elevator in the warehouse took them most of the way up to the residential floor, and then it was just one more staircase to get them to the room they were staying in that night.

Gibson had asked him whether Stasia would need a room of her own, but Owen had said they would be sharing. He wasn't letting his mate get away from him.

It was only a full size bed, rather than a queen, and the fit would be tight, but they would make it work. Owen closed the door with a kick and sat Stasia down on the bed. And in the time it took him to turn back around flick the light on and then return she had half of her clothes off and was starting to wriggle out of her pants.

His eyes snagged on the bandage on her shoulder and he growled at the thought of anyone else sinking their fangs into her.

He could kill Vega for that. For daring to harm his mate.

"Holy shit, how the fuck did I miss it?" Stasia's question pulled him out of his anger.

"What?" he demanded in a rumbly growl.

She finished shucking her pants and knelt on the bed, completely nude and confident in her nakedness. She reached out and tugged on his arm until he was close and she cupped his cheek. "Your eyes have been changing color. And I think your teeth are sharper. I thought it was just a trick of the light. But this is the werewolf thing, isn't it?"

The first time Owen caught it happening it had

freaked him out, but now he understood it was just his wolf trying to get closer to their mate. "Does it scare you?" he asked.

"Should it?" she shot back.

"I would never hurt you."

They kissed again. Owen managed to get his own clothes off and laid Stasia down. She'd said the shoulder didn't hurt, but he was determined to be gentle and care for her like she deserved.

He kissed his way down her stomach and spread her legs so she was open before him. He wanted to feast. And he did, tongue lapping at her sex and groaning in pleasure as she squirmed around him.

One of her hands carded her fingers through his hair and guided him exactly where she wanted. His Stasia didn't give up control. It was one of the most God damn sexy things about her.

Everything was sexy about her.

But Owen was determined to show her that he knew exactly what she needed, and he wasn't going to stop until she was screaming in pleasure.

His tongue swirled and dove into all of her private areas, and when she gasped out his name, he took it for the encouragement that it was.

Her hips bucked against his face as she gave herself over with abandon to the pleasure, and it didn't take long for those screams and cries to start.

He was as hard as iron just from her taste and her smell and the way she sounded, and when he guided himself to her entrance and pushed inside, he couldn't stop the groan of pleasure as her tight heat enveloped him.

Taking it slow was torture, but the kind of torture a man reveled in. Their eyes locked, and he didn't know if it was a trick of the light or something more sinister, but he thought he saw something shift in Stasia's eyes.

Her wolf?

Something else?

But it was gone in a blink, and then they were moving together in a dance as old as time itself. And soon her body rippled around him and that was all it took for Owen to join her in ecstasy.

CHAPTER TWENTY-THREE

STASIA FELT a little bit like a thief in the night, or, well, the morning, as she snuck out of the room she and Owen had shared. He'd clung to her all night and she'd cuddled against him like he was a giant teddy bear. It was nice. Nicer than nice. Cuddling had never been a requirement in a relationship before, but with Owen she never wanted to let go.

But she didn't want to wake him when he was sleeping so peacefully. She pulled on her clothes and considered changing the bandage over the bite mark. She poked at it with two fingers to check.

It felt a bit like an old bruise, a little achy, but not super painful. It should have felt worse.

She decided to leave the bandage as it was. She didn't want to pull it away and find that she had magically healed, a sure sign that she was turning into a werewolf, if there was such a thing as a sure sign. She still wasn't sure if she had imagined the miraculously healing scalpel wound that happened at the same time as the bite.

As long as she didn't think about things too hard, she wasn't going to freak out.

She followed the hallway to a staircase, and then she followed her nose to the smell of pancakes and bacon.

Andre, Leland Rowe, and Em were all in the kitchen with plates of food in front of them. It seemed like everyone had decided to stay over last night.

Stasia's cheeks heated.

Had they heard her and Owen going at it? Werewolf stories and TV shows said they had super senses, enhanced hearing and smell, and maybe even sight. And she and Owen had *not* been quiet.

She clamped her mouth shut. She wasn't going to say a peep about that, and hopefully no one would say anything in return. That was the polite thing to do.

Andre was glowering at Rowe and Em, who were talking quietly on one side of a large table. Stasia found two platters, one with pancakes and one with bacon, and served herself on the assumption the food had been prepared for everyone.

As she got closer, she could tell that Rowe and Em were speaking about a band that Stasia didn't know anything about.

Good for Em. Stasia loved her sister, but she wasn't nearly as into music as Em was. It was good that she could find someone to talk about her interests with. Most people got a bit starstruck around Em and couldn't have a normal conversation. Rowe didn't seem to have that problem. Maybe he didn't know who she was. Maybe he didn't care. Whatever it was, Stasia was glad her sister had made a friend.

But why was Andre glaring? Was he one of the assholes who thought her sister's music wasn't complex enough? Did he think that she didn't deserve her fame? Was he sneering at the conversation? Or at Rowe?

Em worked hard for everything she had. Stasia had seen a lot of it firsthand. In the middle of a tour her sister was bound to collapse from exhaustion, but she always demanded that she keep going. And if Andre couldn't respect that they were going to have words.

Stasia took a seat at the table right next Andre, ready to ream him out if need be. He gave her a tight smile and then looked down at his food, but at least he was no longer glaring at Em and Rowe.

A minute later, Bryan Vega walked inside. He had a bounce in his step and was all smiles, but the smile wiped off his face when he saw Stasia, replaced by a look of remorse. He didn't look like a man who had been shot the day before. And she didn't know a werewolf could look sheepish. "Hi," he offered.

"Good morning," said Stasia. Maybe she should have been angry at him, but he looked scared of her.

He was the werewolf in the situation. She should have been the one that was scared. Right now it didn't look like he could hurt a fly. And Stasia knew he hadn't been in his right mind. She'd worked on patients like that before, the kind who were in so much pain or in such an altered mental state that they had no idea what they were doing. They didn't mean to lash out at their doctors. And holding it against them would just make things worse.

"I'm so sorry," said Vega, all apology as the words poured out of him. "Are you okay? How are you feeling? Can I get you breakfast? Do you need coffee?" The questions ran out of his mouth so quickly she could barely make sense of them.

Stasia tapped her fork against her plate and had to hold back a smile. Vega was young, probably in his mid-twenties, and had the kind of boyish charm that let some men get away with murder. "I'm good. Thanks for offering. And I'm okay. We're good."

But Vega was frozen where he stood and the others stopped talking. Everyone was looking at her as if they expected her to freak out.

Yesterday she might have. And she hated to think that sex had solved the whole thing, but she did feel a lot more relaxed today. Besides, there was nothing she could do. She had been bitten by a werewolf. Maybe she was turning into one. Maybe it would happen in three months. Maybe it would happen in three hours. Maybe it wouldn't happen at all. No one knew.

Was it scary? Yes.

Did she hate not knowing what was going to happen? Of course.

But right now she needed to just accept it.

"It's okay," she repeated. "It's not like you guys have a manual for this. We'll figure it out." She was used to being a steady voice in the hospital, but that didn't mean she was normally the voice of reason. She just wanted things to go back to normal, for some value of normal, as soon as possible.

It took them all a few seconds to accept her words, but Vega went and got his own food and Em and Rowe eventually continued their conversation.

"You're taking this in stride," Andre said to her. He was watching Rowe as if he expected the man to do something, but Stasia didn't know what.

"What are my other options?" she asked him, and meant it.

Andre didn't have a response to that.

She sensed a change in the air and wasn't surprised when Owen walked through the door. His face broke out into a big smile when he saw her and he crossed directly to the table and gave her a thorough kiss.

Stasia kissed him back without hesitation, but when he pulled back she was a bit thrown off. She had never been one for public displays of affection before, and wasn't Owen still technically her bodyguard? The suddenness of the kiss had been enough to overcome any initial hesitation, but she was dealing with a lot at the moment. But Owen kissed really well, and she didn't want him to stop.

"Good morning," he said, his hand running through her hair, grinning at her like they were the only two people in the world.

"Good morning." Why was her voice so high? What was he doing to her?

When she finally remembered that other people were in the room, she looked around and saw Vega, Rowe, and Andre all giving Owen huge grins, and she was sure there was some sort of teasing just about to erupt. Em looked just as pleased.

"So we're at the PDA portion of our relationship?"

The question popped out without her meaning to ask.

Relationship. Was that what this was?

She didn't know what word to put on it, and she was kind of worried to take a step too far. What if this was all werewolf hormones? It didn't feel like something that was going to burn out in a few days or weeks or ever, but everything was still so new.

Owen's grin got huge. "You said relationship." He kissed her again.

Stasia groaned, and it wasn't in pleasure. "Go get your food." She gave him a playful shove and he backed away to grab pancakes and bacon of his own.

Boyfriend. Bodyguard. Something more?

There was a word at the edge of her consciousness, one summoned by all of the werewolf shit, and she wondered if that was the right one.

Was it possible that Owen was her mate?

CHAPTER TWENTY-FOUR

STASIA EXCUSED herself to use the restroom, and Owen managed to stay in his seat for an entire minute before following her into the hallway. He knew she couldn't want him trailing after her every minute, and he considered it a great show of restraint when he merely waited in the hall for her to come back rather than following her and waiting outside the bathroom door.

He wasn't that attached.

Really.

Stasia raised her eyebrows when she saw him leaning against the wall outside of the kitchen. "What's up?" she asked. She stepped close, letting her fingers brush against his side.

It was a relief, a confirmation that he wasn't the

only one who thought they were too far apart when they weren't touching.

"Just wanted to see you." His wolf felt a bit more settled last night, even if it still felt a bit like there was a second creature living inside of him, rather than the unified person he'd been before meeting Stasia. But if he got to keep her, he was pretty sure he could learn to live with it.

"You've seen me all morning," she pointed out as she leaned even closer so that her front pressed against his.

Owen wrapped his arms around her and pulled her flush against him. No more teasing. "I wanted you all to myself," he confessed. He could have cursed himself for not waking with her. They could have made love again in the sunlight of the morning, spent all day in bed. Or at least stayed there for as long as the others allowed it before bothering them. A few hours, definitely.

"Are you turning into mister possessive?" She smiled as she asked, but he had a feeling that she wouldn't be smiling if he kept it up for long.

Owen had *never* been possessive of anyone in his past. He'd never seen the need for it, no matter how much he cared. He trusted his partners, he knew they were with him because they wanted him. But he'd also never felt so much so fast for a person. It wasn't that he didn't trust Stasia. He'd lay down his soul on her word alone. He just wanted to hold her close and cherish this time for as long as they could keep it.

He cupped her cheek and kissed her, slanting his mouth over hers in a passionate declaration. His whole heart was in it, saying words with his actions that he couldn't yet voice.

And Stasia met him where he was, her tongue tangling with his as if they'd been made for each other.

Mate.

The word came naturally now, something to be cherished rather than fought against. Being turned into a werewolf had brought plenty of confusion, but Owen was no longer confused about this, about Stasia. She *was* his mate, whatever that meant and however it turned out. The wolf knew it and now the man accepted it.

He was keeping Stasia forever.

He slid his hands down her sides, holding her tight. He wanted to do more, wanted to strip her bare and slide into her again. He wanted to mark her so the whole world knew she belonged to him.

His fangs ached to shift, even as he kept his human form. Just a little nip, just enough to make the bond whole.

And if she had fangs and fur of her own, she

could mark him as well.

Owen's cock swelled at the thought. She could be his mate in every way, his companion forever, and understand him like no one else. Was it selfish to want that? To celebrate that her life had been completely upended as she was dragged into his world?

She nipped at his lip and Owen groaned.

He thrust against her and it was its own kind of torture. They couldn't start anything here. Half of the team was only a few feet away and anyone could walk down the hall at any time. He didn't want them seeing him taking his mate, but the threat of exposure added desperate heat to the kiss.

He had to stop, but he couldn't. Not when her mouth was just as eager as he was.

He could almost smell her lust. His sense of smell in human form wasn't as sharp as it was when he was a wolf, but it was sharper, and he recognized all of Stasia's wants, or he was beginning to, and he was going to make it his life's work to know her every secret.

It was his job as her mate.

It wouldn't take much to drag her to an unoccupied room and have his way with her. He was sure she'd go with him. But it was hard to remember the layout of the offices when his mind was so focused on Stasia.

No matter how desperate he was, he didn't want to accidentally fuck in Gibson's office. That would be bad.

A sound tickled the edge of his senses, and it wasn't coming from his mate.

Footsteps. Coming closer. He didn't know whose.

Reluctantly Owen pulled away, but he couldn't tear his eyes off Stasia's swollen lips and mussed hair. There was no question that she'd been thoroughly kissed, and no doubt about who'd done it.

He grinned with dark, male satisfaction.

"Caveman," she said with a shake of her head and a fond smile.

He loved that smile, wanted to see more of it. Owen beat his hands against his chest like a cartoon character before leaning down and catching a quick, sweet kiss, forcing himself to pull away before it got any hotter. "Want to see my club?"

That startled a laugh out of her. "Oh god, I should dump you for that." She pushed him away, putting space between them even as she smiled, almost against her will, at his dumb joke.

"You're not getting rid of me." It was both a promise and a threat.

Stasia rolled her eyes. "Come on, let's get back

inside. Otherwise they're going to think we snuck away for a quickie."

"We still could." Owen nodded down the hall. He was mostly joking, but his cock was one hundred percent into the quickie idea.

"Come on, caveman." She tugged on his arm and led him back towards the kitchen.

CHAPTER TWENTY-FIVE

THE MEMORY of the kiss was still fresh on her swollen lips as Stasia sat back down at the kitchen table. Owen came in a moment later and everyone gave them knowing looks. Yeah, there was no hiding what they had been doing. But maybe they didn't need to hide.

It was exhilarating to think about. She'd never had someone truly worthy of the title of *partner* before, but maybe Owen was that guy. Maybe she could count on him for good.

Maybe this time she wouldn't get hurt.

Owen sat down right beside her and she expected a razzing from the guys, but they didn't say anything. Good.

She didn't know them well. Not yet. And she really didn't want to deal with whatever teasing normally went down. After all, these were a bunch of former military guys who only knew how to show affection through insults and swear words.

She didn't want them teasing her yet; that was something only close friends—and sisters—got to do. Even then, it was only Em out of all of her sisters that even tried. Tabitha, Ally, and Heidi didn't try and Emmy was only three.

Maybe one day these guys would be her friends. Maybe she was turning into a werewolf and would soon be a member of the pack, but not today.

Her phone rang and she wanted to ignore it, but she checked the caller ID and saw it was her father. That was a rare enough occurrence that she had to wonder if something was wrong. He didn't take time out from his world domination schemes for just anything.

Had something happened with the kidnappers? Had they missed one? Was she still in danger? Did she still need Owen to be her bodyguard?

It was strange how much she wanted the answer to the last question to be a yes. A week ago and she had fought against it with all her might. Now she couldn't imagine letting him go.

She was a bit frantic as she answered. "What's up? Is everything okay?" She didn't waste time with hellos. Her father was too busy to care for them.

But Armand Selby continued to be full of surprises. "I just got the guest list for Emmy's birthday party. Why aren't you on it?" he demanded, with the same kind of force he would use while negotiating a contract between warring nations.

Stasia had to pull the phone away from her ear and look at the screen to make sure she wasn't being pranked. But the number belonged to her father. And the voice sounded like him. She put the phone back up to her ear. "Are you kidding? I'm not going. I almost got kidnapped, doesn't that give me a break?" And hadn't she had this exact conversation with AR? What was it with Emmy's birthday? None of her other siblings had ever been celebrated so much.

Beside her she could hear Owen growl, and she reached out a hand to place it on his thigh to calm him down.

"You are a Selby and you need to be there," her father pressed, as if this was more than a child's party. It wasn't. Sometimes her dad got a stick up his ass and decided to make a stand. Apparently Emmy's birthday was one of those times.

Her life was Selby bullshit and she didn't need it. Cancer had stolen her mother away, but Stasia carried her name for a reason. "I'm a Nichols and I will do whatever the hell I want." And then she did something she had never done before in her life: she hung up on her father.

It felt good.

All of the guys were looking at her with curiosity in their eyes and Em had a huge grin on her face.

"Good for you, sis," she said. If she'd been close enough, Stasia was sure she would have reached over and hugged her.

"I should have done that a long time ago." She loved her father, even if the relationship was a bit complicated. But he didn't get to run her life. Not even when it came to something as inconsequential as a toddler's birthday party.

"What's that all about?" asked Rowe. He looked the most confused out of all of them. Andre seemed like he was interested but trying not to be, while Vega seemed to be holding still, as if Stasia might forget that he was there. Owen didn't look confused at all. Of course, he already had the story.

There was no use hiding it, and with every retelling Stasia found it kind of funny. "Our baby sister is having a birthday party pretty soon. Emmy. She's turning three. And everyone is trying to put together the guest list." It sounded so inconsequential when she said it like that.

Rowe looked between Em and Stasia, but it was

Andre who spoke. "Em and Emmy?" he asked. "What is that? Emma and Emerald? Sounds confusing."

Em's grin turned into a glare, and she took the explanation from Stasia. "We're both named Emerald. Dad lets our moms choose our names. He's had six wives. And ten children. He forgot to mention to Riley, our 23-year-old stepmother, that my actual name is Emerald, so she named her own kid Emerald. It's super fun."

Rowe clamped his mouth shut as if he had to keep from laughing while Andre had an unreadable look on his face. Vega was still doing his statue routine. Owen already knew the story so luckily he wasn't reacting in a way likely to get him on Em's dark side.

"I know it's fucked up. It's okay," said Stasia. The guys looked like they were liable to break something if they kept holding back their expressions. "We're just as screwed up as any rich family that has a reality show about them. We just don't let cameras into our houses."

"So your dad is still having this big party with you at risk of being kidnapped?" asked Owen.

Stasia glanced at Owen. She had mentioned that the kidnapping threat was gone, but clearly he hadn't said anything to anyone else yet.

She couldn't lie about it. "I'm sure that my father

would be more than willing to have a party while we were all at risk of kidnapping if it was what it took to keep up appearances. But AR let me know that his people have identified the threat and are in the process of rounding them up. That's why I don't have an extra team tailing me anymore. It's all good now." She still had her hand on Owen's thigh and his muscles clenched under her fingers.

She didn't know what to say to reassure him that she wasn't about to walk away. She didn't need him just because he was her bodyguard. She wanted him for far more than that. She wanted to keep him around for good.

But before she could figure out how to say that, Hunter stuck her head into the room. "Hey, guys, Gibson wants to talk to all of us. The team. Stasia and Em will need to keep themselves entertained for about an hour. Come on."

That stopped conversation. Apparently when Gibson said jump, his team started hopping.

Owen gave her a resounding kiss before he and his colleagues left her and Em alone in the room.

Stasia wished that a toddler's birthday party was the most of her worries.

CHAPTER TWENTY-SIX

GIBSON WAS WAITING with the rest of the team as Willa led them into the conference room and took a seat beside Vega and Rowe. Owen and Andre took seats on the other side of the table. Gibson was at the head with Jackson beside him.

He gave Owen a long stare before turning and nodding to greet everyone else. That was kind of weird. Owen wanted to say something, but he didn't know what.

Everything felt new again, and not necessarily in a good way. He felt wrong-footed, just like he'd felt two years ago after the ritual had been performed on all of them. He didn't know what was happening, he didn't understand it, and he wasn't sure he ever could. He only hoped Gibson could shed some light on the subject.

Gibson had a laptop in front of him and projector set up to project onto the white wall at the front of the conference room. He pulled up some pictures and had them on display. "Does somebody want to tell me what went wrong on Vega and Rowe's job?" he asked with deceptive calm.

That was how their debriefs always started. Though usually the job didn't go wrong. Usually no one got shot.

Vega hung his head and stiffened his shoulders. "We got lazy," Rowe said with a hint of defiance in his voice. "We thought the job was over and we were coasting. And Vega almost got killed."

"Are you going to do it again?" Gibson asked.

Both Vega and Rowe shook their heads, followed by the rest of the team also shaking their heads. They might not have been there, but it could just as easily have been them.

"I expect a full write up by morning. You may need to give statements to the police. We will have to do something about Vega's alleged injury if that happens. But I'm glad you're alive." And that ended that portion of the meeting. Normally it went longer. Normally Gibson would have brought up photos from every angle and had them walk the team through the entire job. They were still pretty new to this bodyguarding gig and every job was a learning experience.

But today they had something bigger to talk about.

"How is Stasia doing?" Gibson asked him.

Owen didn't want to answer. His loyalty to Stasia warred with his loyalty to Gibson. But he knew that Stasia and Gibson were on the same side. Gibson only wanted to help. And he couldn't help if he didn't know what was going on. "She's doing well," he said. "Freaked out a bit. But she seems pretty accepting. Maybe resigned is the right word. She says that whatever happens, happens."

It was more complicated than that, he knew. But Owen could really only report what she had told him. And he believed her. So what more was there to say?

"Chip is acting weird, right?" Vega asked, using the nickname he'd earned back in the Army. It was meant to be a jokey name, but now was not the time for jokes. "This is like more than a job to you." It stood on the line between teasing and accusation, and Owen had to bite back a growl and keep himself from lunging toward Vega.

Andre was looking at him as if he expected him to pounce. He didn't know if his friend would hold them back or back him up. "Do you think she's going to turn into a wolf?" Rowe added.

Owen couldn't stop the growl this time.

Gibson ignored Owen's reaction. "No way to know. But I've been waiting for something like this to happen for a while. I've been tracking us since we first turned. Trying to keep a record of our symptoms and our reactions, the things that have changed since *we* changed. I'm not a doctor or scientist, but even I can see that we're becoming… More. Different. I don't think our first change was the end of things for us."

"What do you mean?" asked Andre, sitting straighter in his seat.

Owen wondered what he meant, too. And did it have anything to do with what his eyes and his teeth were doing?

"We've all become more controlled over our wolf forms then we were in those first couple of months. And everyone is lifting stronger weights in human form than any of us were back in the military. And I think some of our wolfishness is bleeding into our humanity, just as our humanity is bleeding into our wolves. Does that sound right?" He looked right at Owen as he asked the last part.

It did. It sounded almost scarily familiar. "I think my eyes shifted when I was in human form. Teeth too," Owen admitted. He didn't need to hide this from his people. They were his team, his pack, and he trusted them.

Gibson nodded as if this wasn't a surprise, but he made a note of something on his computer. "Anyone else?" he asked.

Jackson raised her hand. "I managed to summon my claws in human form. Once. I haven't been able to do it again." She looked a little sheepish as she said it, as if she couldn't believe that she was playing around with her powers.

Gibson made another note. "So what do we do about Stasia?" asked Hunter, her arms crossed. "We all decided to keep the whole werewolf thing a secret."

"It's a little late for that," Andre muttered.

"What can we do?" asked Rowe. "Stasia and Em know now. And we can't exactly take that knowledge away from them."

They all looked around at each other, as if some magical solution would make itself known. It didn't.

"We wait and see what happens to Owen's mate," Gibson finally declared.

Owen startled as if stung. That word had been knocking around in his own head for the past few days but it was strange to hear Gibson say it.

"Mate?" Andre asked, all incredulity.

"Seems so," said Gibson. He looked at Owen, giving him the opportunity to contradict him. When Owen kept quiet, Gibson continued. "One of those changes I was talking about."

Owen didn't argue, but he also didn't add his own thoughts. That was too raw to share.

"What about the sister?" asked Rowe. "Do we have to bite her?" Owen wasn't sure if Rowe was joking. "And doesn't she look familiar?"

Andre made a noise in the back of his throat that might have been a growl, but he didn't say anything.

"No shit she looks familiar," said Hunter, surprising Owen. "She won a freaking Grammy last year." He didn't know Hunter followed music that closely.

"No shit?" Rowe looked impressed. Owen realized that Rowe didn't know who Em was. They descended into discussion of Em's music career for several minutes until Gibson called them back to order. "If yesterday taught us anything, it's that we need someone with medical training. We don't know what would have happened to Vega. Maybe it would be a good idea to have a doctor with us full-time. Something for Stasia to consider."

Owen liked the sound of that.

But he wondered if Stasia would be willing to stay.

CHAPTER TWENTY-SEVEN

STASIA ENDED up back in the room she'd shared with Owen the night before. She wished he were there with her, and she had no idea how much longer she had to wait until his meeting was over. And then she kind of hated how she was waiting for him. Who was she becoming? She didn't need a man. She didn't need to depend on anyone but herself.

But that didn't mean she couldn't want Owen.

Before she could get too caught up in her thoughts, her phone rang, and thankfully this time it wasn't her father or any of her siblings. "Hey, Luna. What's up?" The nurse didn't normally call her, but it was good to hear from a friend. It was a reminder that the outside world still existed, one without werewolves or kidnappers or toddler's birthday parties.

"I got the job," Luna said with excitement. "You remember the one I told you about the other day?"

It took Stasia a second to remember. It felt like a lifetime ago, even if it was slightly less than a week. But then she did. "Congratulations!" She was happy for her friend, even if that meant they wouldn't see each other at the clinic anymore.

If Stasia was going back to the clinic.

Could she be a werewolf and a doctor at the same time? What kind of complications would that bring up? She had the strangest image of operating on someone while her hands were sporting claws.

"They're looking for doctors," said Luna. "I want to give them your name. I think you would be perfect for this place."

Stasia probably should have said yes without any hesitation. She couldn't spend the rest of her life working at a free clinic. Well, she could, but she didn't know if that would be fulfilling enough. Getting back into an emergency room would be high-stakes. Exhilarating. She'd be saving lives every day.

Was that what she wanted?

A week ago she probably would have said yes. But an entire new world had opened up to her, and now she was filled with curiosity of a shape-shifting variety.

"You still there?" Luna asked.

Stasia realized she had been quiet for too long. "I'm still here. I need to think about it before you give them my name. It's been a really busy week."

"Okay." Luna didn't sound too disappointed, but she normally was peppy enough. "You owe me drinks. And I expect a call back. I don't care that we're not working together anymore. We're still friends."

"I promise," and Stasia meant it. She had a feeling she was going to need someone normal, someone who knew nothing about the werewolf world, to ground her as her life was changing. And Luna was just the person for that.

The door to the bedroom opened just as Stasia said goodbye and hung up the phone. Owen wrapped his arms around her tight and Stasia felt some of her tension melt away.

"Did you hear that?" she asked. He might have been outside the room and she wasn't sure just how sharp his hearing was. Now that she knew he wasn't completely human she had to wonder what exactly he could do.

"Nope," he said. They rocked back and forth a bit as if swaying to music that wasn't playing.

"My friend Luna got a job at a new hospital. She invited me to apply for a position there. They're looking for doctors. It would probably be a good fit."

It sounded like she was trying to justify it to herself. Why didn't it feel right anymore? It wasn't just the werewolf stuff. Stasia had been adrift for a while, ever since she left her last job. She hadn't been sure it was right then, and she didn't know if it was right now.

"Do you want to go back to a hospital?" Owen asked gently. It was clear he was not trying to influence the decision. It would be so easy if he did try and influence it.

"I don't know," she admitted. "It should be right up my alley. It's high-pressure, it's important."

"But it's not what you want," said Owen, plainly stating what she was afraid to confess.

"No, it's not what I want." It was strange and freeing to admit that. It was something she had been dancing around for quite some time. She had spent so long and worked so hard to earn her qualifications and to get jobs where she would truly make a difference. But it didn't satisfy her anymore. It wasn't right. Not anymore.

"You know we could always use a doctor." Owen offered. "You saved Vega's life. And you could probably tell us a lot about what's going on in our bodies that we don't understand. I can't guarantee it will pay much, but it'll be interesting."

It was almost too good to be true. Stasia's heart

beat a little faster and her mind whirred with possibilities. A doctor to werewolves. No one else had that kind of opportunity. "Is this you asking me? Or Gibson?" She didn't know which one she wanted to be offering her the job. She didn't want Owen to offer her out of pity or out of some weird effort to keep her close, but she also liked the idea that it would be Owen thinking of it instead of his boss. Even as her mind warred against it, her heart wanted him to want her close.

"Gibson suggested it," Owen admitted. "But I think you would be great at it. I want you here. But if I was making up a job for you it would involve a lot more sexual favors," he added.

A surprised laugh burst out of Stasia. "I'll probably throw in the sexual favors for free."

She wasn't ready to make the decision. Not yet. No matter how intriguing doctor to werewolves sounded, she had some thinking to do. Then Owen kissed her and she decided that she could think later.

CHAPTER TWENTY-EIGHT

OWEN COULDN'T RESIST KISSING Stasia. Every moment they were apart was too long, and he and his wolf were in agreement on that. The thought of her staying with them, working with them, only added fire to his blood. She hadn't said yes. She might not say yes. But the possibility was there now.

There was no telling what the future held for them, but now they had a chance to seize it.

Stasia wrapped her legs around his waist as he leaned against the wall and held her in place, his cock hardening to steel as he pressed against her.

"Yes," his mate groaned, deepening their kiss.

Owen's mind was in a haze of lust as he flashed through all the things he could do to her, all the things they could do together. He wanted to steal her away and lock them both up in a tower somewhere so that no one would find them. The more barbaric part of his mind imagined chaining her to the bed, but as she nipped at his lip the fantasy changed until *he* was the one in manacles and Stasia was having her way with him.

Yes.

Both.

Either.

Whatever happened, so long as it was with her.

At points in his past he'd worried about finding someone to stand by forever. He'd thought he'd feel cramped, limited. But now his mind was completely focused on Stasia and there was no limitation. She was all he wanted. All he would ever want.

Mate.

The thought was music to his ears.

He swung her around and sat her gently on the bed.

"I'm not fragile, you know," Stasia said with heat as she tore off her top and tossed it across the room.

"I know." Owen made quick work of his own top and unbuttoned his jeans, but he didn't get them all the way off. Stasia was right there and far too tempting. He knelt between her legs and began kissing every inch of exposed skin, paying special attention to her breasts when she moaned as his tongue swirled around a nipple. "Not fragile at all," he said between kisses. "But precious. Mine."

She moaned again before threading her fingers through her hair and surprising him with a countermove right out of a jiu-jitsu studio, using her hips to thrust up and flip him over. She straddled his waist, her hair hanging over them like a curtain. "Yours?" There was a challenge in her eyes.

Another man might have treaded carefully, but Owen was one with his wolf and he knew it was time to prove to their mate just where she belonged. "Absolutely. Forever."

And if she thought she was going to best him with a move like that, she was mistaken. She had a few tricks up her sleeve, but he was a trained soldier and bodyguard. And he was claiming her.

Owen sat up and gripped Stasia close, crushing their mouths together in a branding kiss. He flipped them back over so he was on top, his full body covering Stasia's and holding her in place. She didn't seem to mind as she wrapped her arms and legs around him and kissed him for all she was worth.

He needed to be inside her. His cock throbbed in desperation and he could practically feel the tight press of her wet heat, but no force in the universe was strong enough to pull him back from kissing her.

He let his hands roam over her silky skin and

took pride in her shiver as she fell deeper into the kiss. And when they rolled the next time Owen didn't even think to fight it. This wasn't really a battle of wills. There was no need to tame or conquer.

They were in this thing together.

"You're mine too, you know," Stasia panted when they finally separated for a moment.

"That was never in doubt." There were more words to say, another declaration even stronger to make, but Owen held it back. Between the bite and the other revelations, it was far too much too soon.

He'd wait.

Until at least tomorrow.

But right now he needed something more physical. He kissed his way down Stasia's body again, and this time when he made it to her pants he started to pull them off. They managed to get tangled and Stasia's curse at the complication almost had him laughing.

His mate had a rough edge to her, a side always willing to fight, but she was aligned with him and he reveled in it. His teeth ached along with his fingers and he could feel his wolf rising to the surface.

No.

He tried to pull the change back. This was something human, something just between him and

Stasia, and he wouldn't scare her by letting his other half take over.

We are one, his wolf whispered to him.

Were they really? Kind of hard to think that was true when he was imagining the creature speaking to him.

He didn't want to pull back from Stasia, but with the wolf so close to the surface, so determined to claim her, he feared that he would go too far. She'd accepted the wolf stuff but there had to be a limit. And a part of him would die inside if the limit came from him.

He pulled back and sat up, turning away from Stasia and breathing deep, trying to center himself. He was a man. He was with his woman. There was no need for the wolf to get involved.

But he could still feel it, lurking. It made no move to recede, no matter how much he tried to pull himself together. If anything, he was making it worse. His hand shook as he tried to run it through his hair, and when he brought it back down he saw his nails sharpening into claws.

It couldn't have taken more than a few moments, but Stasia sat up, knowing something was wrong.

"Let me see you," she said. "I'm here."

CHAPTER TWENTY-NINE

Stasia sat up and placed her hand on Owen's cheek to turn his head towards hers. He resisted for a moment and then let her move him. When she caught sight of his eyes she almost gasped. They'd gone that same wolfish yellow she'd seen before, and she could almost swear she saw fangs peeking out of his mouth.

"Why are you trying to hide from me?" she asked. Maybe the sight of his wolf so close to the surface should have scared away her lust, but her body was still tight with it. She wasn't about to run away just because she was seeing some of Owen's true self.

Owen turned his head until he could brush a kiss against her palm before he spoke. "You're dealing with enough, you shouldn't need to deal with my lack of control."

"Control?" She couldn't help but smile. She kissed his cheek. He was too close for her to keep from touching and she wasn't even going to try and resist. "You seem pretty controlled to me. Or are you going to let the change go further?"

"How can you look at me and say that?" He sounded wrecked, and Stasia never wanted to hear that tone from him again. Her man was cheerful, confident. He embraced his wolf and his life and didn't get scared because of a few small changes.

She kissed him, careful to avoid the sprouting fangs, but not too careful. And then she deepened the kiss and forgot about the fangs altogether. It was hard to think about anything but Owen when they were naked together.

She pulled back and took a good look at him. "You seem safe enough to me."

"You're not scared?" He still sounded doubtful.

"You're a werewolf. I can stand a little weird. Now come back here and fuck me." The next time she kissed him wasn't as gentle. Owen said he was out of control? She dared him to show her.

He did.

She heard a growl start deep in his throat and it awakened something deep inside her. She didn't know if she had a wolf of her own, but there was definitely a piece of her soul that responded to his and she never wanted it to end.

He tipped her back on the bed and pressed her against the mattress, kissing her like he would brand her. His sharp teeth were there, but he wasn't a vampire and they weren't razor sharp.

Did vampires exist?

The thought was washed away in another wave of lust and Stasia didn't care enough to chase it. Owen's hands raked down her side and he cupped one of her breasts, stroking her nipple with his thumb. She loved the feel of his hands on her and needed more.

Did she have to beg?

Before she could make a noise, his other hand found her entrance and his fingers teased her wet heat, dipping inside and stretching her, making her ready for him.

"Fuck," she groaned. And then something occurred to her. "Fuck! Condom."

Owen stopped moving for a moment and Stasia almost told him to forget about it. She was on birth control, they could take their chances. But after the day they'd had, they didn't need any more surprises.

Luckily, Owen had restocked his wallet and after a minute he was suited up and ready for more.

There was no hesitation now, no concern for

yellow eyes or his wolf rising to the surface. Stasia trusted Owen and knew he'd never hurt her. It was freeing to give herself over to that trust and watch him unleash.

They came together with a desperate ferocity and the sounds they made were completely feral. Stasia had never sounded like that in bed before, but Owen brought the intensity out of her and made everything *more*.

He entered her and they moved, and the pleasure mounted. Stasia was full to the core but she still wanted more. She couldn't quite say what *more* was as she held Owen tight and urged him on.

"I'm yours." The declaration was true deep down in her soul. She'd never be rid of this connection, this impossible bound that had sprung up between them. It was impossible to explain, deeper and truer than emotion.

Her body rippled around his as she came and Owen let out a roar of triumph as he joined her. Then his eyes flashed an even deeper yellow and his fangs got impossibly long.

She didn't have time to be scared as he bit down on her shoulder, marking her as his. She cried out in a mix of pleasure and pain as her vision went white and she passed out.

CHAPTER THIRTY

"I'M FINE, I promise. Stop looking at me like that." The mark that Owen had left on her shoulder wasn't nearly as bad as they feared. In fact, it was already mostly healed, and since Stasia's body still felt delightfully stretched from their lovemaking, she had a feeling there was some sort of magical bullshit contributing to it.

Her werewolf boyfriend bit her. She knew she should be freaking out. That was a freaking out kind of thing. But for some reason she wasn't.

Maybe her quota for freak outs had been used up, or maybe it was something else. She wasn't going to examine it too closely. She was going to consider a lack of panic a good thing for now.

"I'm not looking at it," Owen insisted. He was packing up a few things to take back to her apartment. There wasn't much. They hadn't intended to stay overnight in the first place.

Gibson had offered to let her stay in the safe house until everyone had a better idea of what was going to happen to her, but Stasia had a nice home just a few miles away and she would rather sleep in her own bed.

It had taken Owen and the rest of his pack three months to turn into werewolves; she wasn't going to stay in Brooklyn that long if she could avoid it. And there was half a chance she wouldn't turn into a werewolf at all. They didn't have a way to measure it, so all she could go on was instinct and her knowledge of her own body.

She was trying to decide if she felt any different. Her stomach felt a little upset, but the only meals she had eaten for the past day and a half were greasy fast food. Anxiety mixed with fat and grease was a particularly sickly combination. It was no sure sign of lycanthropy.

Stasia had finally gathered up the courage to look at the bite mark that Vega had left, and it was already healed enough to get rid of the stitches. She had taken them out herself without asking for help.

It was another sign that she was likely turning into a werewolf. An upset stomach could be anything. Healing from a wound that big so fast?

There was nothing human about that. Was she dealing with the trauma by avoiding the possibility? Yes. But she figured she had at least a few days—maybe months—to get her mind wrapped around the situation.

She had put a fresh bandage over the bite just so it didn't raise questions from the other guys. Maybe it was stupid to keep that from them, but she was entitled to a bit of stupidity for at least a day. She hadn't even told Owen and knew he'd hold it against her, but she just needed a bit more time. He'd understand. Right?

Em knocked on the door and Owen answered it. "I need to take off," she said as she entered the room and got close to Stasia. She looked regretful. "My manager has been blowing up my phone. I was hoping I could buy a couple more days, but it doesn't look like it. Are you going to be okay? Because I will cancel the tour and do whatever I need if you want me to stay." Stasia recognized sincerity when she heard it, and Em meant every word she said.

But it wasn't something Stasia could ask of her. That tour cost millions of dollars and there were thousands of fans that would be disappointed if she backed out at this point. And that had nothing on what kind of speculation there would be in the press. She couldn't do that to her sister. "I'm doing fine. I will let you know if anything happens. I promise." It wasn't even a lie. Not exactly. She had no way to know what was happening or when.

"And she has me," Owen added. He was her silent watcher, done with the bag but still there, ready to stand at her side as long as she wanted him.

The *other* healed over bite burned at the thought, but it didn't hurt. It was a reassurance that Owen was there, a steady presence she could always count on.

Em nodded at him and then gave Stasia a hug. It was a relief to know her sister didn't hesitate to get close to her even though she could turn into a furry monster at any moment. Stasia flashed back to an hour before when she'd been taming her own monster and Owen's bite tingled again. Maybe their family didn't have a healthy sense of survival, after all.

"I love you," said Em, hugging her again. "And you better call me. Werewolf or not. That shit is cool. I want to know more." She gave Stasia a kiss on the cheek and took off.

Stasia sank down onto the bed and let out a breath. Maybe the werewolf shit was cool from the outside, but she was exhausted. "I'm ready to go home. Take me?"

The look Owen gave her was too serious for the moment and his word felt like a vow. "Anywhere."

Leaving the safe house didn't take long. Andre was nowhere to be found and Vega made himself scarce. None of the rest of the pack asked Stasia any probing questions, though she did see Gibson give Owen a significant look. She decided to ask about that later; for now, she just wanted to be gone.

Owen brought the car around and she climbed in to the front seat. The traffic gods blessed them and getting back to her place didn't take too long. But once the car was parked they didn't get out.

Stasia wasn't sure what to do. Momentum had pushed her this far, but now she had actual choices to make. Choices about Owen and her and what they really meant to one another.

Owen's stuff was inside, so he had to go in to at least get that, but he wasn't her bodyguard anymore. She was supposed to be safe. Whatever bad guys were after her were supposed to be taken care of.

She wasn't sure that she had the full story, but she didn't think that her brother or her father would purposely put her in peril. Use her as bait? Maybe, but even if they were doing that, they would warn her.

Right?

That was something she shouldn't dwell on.

"I can stay," Owen offered as he looked over at

her, one hand on the steering wheel, one on the console between them.

"As my bodyguard or my boyfriend?" After the nights they'd spent together and all that they shared, it felt a little strange to ask, but she needed to be sure. Owen had made his declarations, and they sure as hell liked each other. Their chemistry was off the charts.

Owen leaned across the car and gave her a searing kiss. When he pulled back he was grinning. "Does that answer your question?"

She couldn't help but touch her fingers to her lips. "It's been a long time since I've had a boyfriend. None of them have been like you. And I don't think I've ever dated a werewolf. I'm not really good at the dating thing." It was probably a little late to warn him about her less than stellar dating record. But it only seemed fair.

"I can be a lot more than your boyfriend," Owen said, undeterred by her warning. "I want to keep you forever."

Her heart leapt, but she wasn't surprised. Everything between them was so intense. Maybe it would be good to test out what it was like to be with him without werewolf bullshit or kidnappers threatening them every minute.

But still Stasia had to tease him a little.

"So we have sex a few times and suddenly I'm your fated mate?" she asked with a grin. The weight of the last week was lifting off of her and she could imagine what it would be like to just *be* with Owen.

But Owen froze where he sat, eyes wide. "What did you say?" he asked carefully.

That wasn't the reaction she was expecting. "Isn't that what all of these stories say? You're a werewolf. Silver hurts you. Of course you have a fated mate. But I don't belong to you." She wanted to be absolutely clear on that point. "No matter what I said in the heat of the moment. I'm not about to be a little woman. Got that?"

Owen gave a shell-shocked nod, and then he leaned in again and kissed her, and this time it was even more passionate than the last.

"Fated mate. I like the sound of that." He grinned.

They went inside but they didn't make it very far before Owen scooped her up off of her feet and charged up the stairs to her bedroom, slamming the door behind them.

CHAPTER THIRTY-ONE

APPREHENSION HAD BEEN GROWING within Owen for a few hours. Stasia was safely upstairs asleep, but he was doing a final check to make sure all of the doors were locked and that the security system was engaged. It was near midnight and he wished the security team was still outside.

Was this the kind of fear that came from loving someone? Was he always going to worry that someone might come for his mate?

Or would he be better once he was convinced that the kidnappers who had wanted her really were gone?

He would ask Stasia if he could talk to her father and brother the next day. Perhaps AR or Armand Selby could give him some insight into what was going on. He wasn't going to let anyone come for Stasia again.

The security system was engaged, the doors and windows were locked, and there wasn't much more Owen could do to make sure they were safe. He considered taking a walk around the building to look for anyone suspicious but decided that was a step too far.

He wasn't that paranoid.. But maybe he should have been.

He heard something plonk against the giant windows in the library. The French doors could open to a small balcony and it would make a great point of entrance if someone could get up to this floor. Definitely not impossible given the fire escapes or sufficient climbing equipment.

He checked it out, but the sound didn't seem to be anything. Maybe a bird or a twig. He opened up his senses, trying to use his wolf, but still nothing.

Everything was fine. Stasia was safe. Or as safe as she ever could be.

He headed back toward the bedroom and that was when he heard her scream.

Owen sprinted. Who had her? How had he missed something?

The screams were gut-wrenching. It sounded like she was being stabbed and Owen could feel his claws and teeth growing sharper as he busted through the door, ready to take on whoever was threatening his mate.

But there was no one else inside the bedroom.

Stasia lay on the bed and thrashed from side to side, her body covered in a heavy sweat and her mouth letting out pained screams.

Owen had to take a deep breath to pull in his claws and teeth. His mate needed him for something else. This wasn't an enemy he could fight.

He made it to the side of the bed and wasn't sure whether he should touch her. Finally he decided to at least feel for a fever. That was a first step. His hand covered her forehead and her skin was burning hot.

Her eyes flashed open and they were the same yellow he saw when his wolf was close to the surface.

She was changing. It might've taken him and the others three months to go from the ritual to their first change, but she had only been bitten about a day ago, maybe thirty hours at the most. He knew that was important information, something he would need to know, but it didn't feel important now. Right now he just had to figure out how to get her safely through this.

He and the others had changed quickly once it had begun. There had been howling, but not much screaming, and not this kind of pain.

Was something wrong?

Was this something a person wasn't meant to survive?

Fear swept over Owen and he wished he had somebody he could call, but he wasn't going to leave Stasia alone. She needed someone to bring her through this change and out the other side and that someone was him.

At least that was his plan until he heard glass shatter in another room and the security alarm started blaring.

His instincts had been right. She wasn't safe.

He had his gun still on him and his wolf within him, but how could he leave Stasia?

A second window shattered in another room. That meant more than one intruder. Probably more than two. If he didn't leave to defend her, the intruders might get to her. And she was in such a vulnerable state that she couldn't fight back.

He couldn't leave her in this room. It wasn't easily defensible. And it was the first place that the intruders would check. Besides, he didn't want her to get wrapped up in the sheets as she struggled against the change. He scooped her off of the bed and winced as she let out a pained cry.

She would be okay. She had to be.

The master bathroom only had a small window

to the outside, one a person couldn't fit through. It meant she was trapped, but they would have to get through him to get to her. He placed her in the bathtub. It wasn't safe, but there weren't obstructions there and he didn't have many other choices.

Owen gave her forehead a kiss and then turned away and headed out to fight whoever was coming for her. He was going to show no mercy; they didn't get to come into his mate's home and try to take her or hurt her. It would be the last mistake they ever made.

While his wolf hadn't been much help during his patrol of the house, now it was close to the surface and it felt like he could hear everything, smell everything, even see everything. He was tempted to shift fully, but he needed his hands. Claws and sharp teeth would have to do.

He closed the bathroom door and hoped that it would hold for long enough. Then he left the bedroom.

The first attacker had already made it to the hallway outside the bedroom, and Owen leapt at him without hesitation. The man didn't have a gun. That was good. It meant he probably wasn't here for death, just kidnapping. But that was his mistake. He had a Taser, and it might've done enough to slow

Owen down if he hadn't got the jump on the guy, but he did.

And he made short work of him with teeth and claws and punches. The man went down and Owen didn't care if he was dead or alive. Judging by the amount of blood he didn't have much hope for survival.

One down, how many to go?

He continued down the hall and followed his ears to the next guy. This one had a stun gun and it almost touched Owen, but he was too fast, and this time he reached for his own weapon and got off two shots, making the man drop down.

Two down.

There were still more. At least four if his ears were not deceiving him, and he doubted they were. Six people to come and retrieve Stasia. Overkill? If that's what they thought, they were severely mistaken.

But the arrogance of Owen's wolf almost got him killed. He charged down the hall ready to take on the next attacker, but the four remaining weren't loners. They were bunched together as a solid unit, and judging by their gear were more than capable of taking on one man, even a man as well trained as Owen.

Stasia screamed again. Owen wanted to go to her.

She needed help. She needed her mate. She shouldn't be doing this alone. But if he went to her, she was doomed.

He checked the clip of his gun and took cover, hoping he could get off lucky shots and take these guys out.

One on four were terrible odds, especially since he was wearing street clothes and only had one clip for his gun.

But he had to win. It was the only shot.

Stasia screamed again.

"What's wrong with her?" a male voice demanded, one of the kidnappers.

"We better not have gone through all this trouble for a dead bitch," said another.

Owen growled.

And then he felt something at the back of his consciousness, an awareness that he only felt on nights of the full moon. It wasn't his wolf. It almost felt like someone else's. Two other people.

The front door burst open and the four attackers screamed as a hail of bullets showered them. It was loud enough to drown out Stasia's screams. Andre and Vega entered while the kidnappers took cover.

Andre found Owen quickly. "Go to her. We've got this."

"How did you know to come?" Owen didn't have time to ask, but he had to know.

"Gibson wanted us to watch your back. He had a bad feeling about this."

Gibson was right. Owen didn't waste anymore time talking. He ran up the steps and went to the bedroom and then into the bathroom. Stasia was still screaming and her body looked wrecked, caught between human form and another.

He didn't know how she was going to survive this, but he would sell his soul to make sure that she did.

CHAPTER THIRTY-TWO

THE PAIN WAS TEARING Stasia apart. She screamed, but her mouth made no sound. She would give up anything to have it end. She didn't know it was possible for a person to feel like this.

Was she still alive? It couldn't hurt this much to die. Or was she being sent to some sort of eternal damnation where she was doomed to feel like this for the rest of eternity?

She never thought it would end. The fire ripped through her and rolled around and made it impossible to think.

But between one breath and the next, it did. Something rippled over her and her body shifted, her limbs finding a new shape, fur growing from her skin, and her senses sharpening in a way they had never sharpened before.

Stasia breathed deep and caught scents she didn't know were possible.

Was that blood?

That was a smell she recognized, human or wolf. And that was what she was now, a wolf. The bite had taken hold. She had shifted.

She didn't have time to think about it before the need to move overtook her. She bounced up and realized that she was sitting in her bathtub and Owen was right there beside her. But he was human.

She gave a small bark and watched as his face lit up in joy. She wanted him to shift with her and run, but he just ran his fingers through her hair and said something she couldn't quite understand. Her senses were all firing at once and it was hard to make sense of *anything*.

She climbed out of the bathtub, which took a little bit of work to figure out, and then she pranced into her bedroom, but when she tried to leave the room Owen wouldn't let her. She growled at him, demanding that he move aside, but he said something again and didn't move.

Stasia ran in circles around the room and made herself dizzy. The room had seemed big when she bought the house, but it was still just big by New York standards and she barely had any room to move.

But the burst of energy burned itself out almost as quickly as it came and after only a few minutes, Stasia climbed up onto the bed and collapsed in a tired heap of fur.

She didn't know what the blood smell was. She didn't know why Owen was so scared. But she was too tired to really think about it for long and sleep claimed her. The last thing she felt was Owen combing his fingers through her fur.

She shifted back to human some time in the middle of the night and woke up on the bed, completely naked, but covered by her sheets. She didn't see Owen anywhere but she could hear someone moving around the house. A glance at the clock told her it was early, really early. The sun was barely peeking out through the windows, definitely not fully risen yet, and the normal sounds of the city from outside were muted as they often were in the early morning hours.

Stasia took stock of her body. She was a werewolf. She remembered the pain from the night before and the change, but there was something missing. Her mind had been so focused on what was happening to her, but she could feel an emptiness, something she didn't know. Something that had to do with this scent of blood that was permeating her house.

She stretched her muscles and tried to decide if

she felt much different. There was an awareness in the back of her mind. Her wolf? The pack? Maybe.

But she still felt like herself. She didn't feel like someone who was bound to turn into a raving monster and rampage through the city on the search for fresh blood. She just felt like Stasia Nichols, doctor and werewolf.

Doctor to werewolves?

Maybe that too. But she was pretty sure everyone would give her at least a day to think it over.

Stasia put on clothes and headed downstairs. The first sign of trouble was the blood on the walls. And then there was the broken glass.

Had she done this? She didn't remember moving around. She remembered Owen blocking the door after she shifted. Had she rampaged through the house before the change took hold?

But a few steps more showed more blood and it definitely wasn't hers. If she had lost that much blood she would have known it.

There was a draft coming down the hallway and she took a few steps toward the office before Owen stepped in her path.

"Come on. We've got some decisions to make."

"Decisions?" She didn't like the sound of that. She wanted to know what had happened. But Owen was going to tell her and she just had to follow him for now.

She was surprised to see Vega and Andre sitting at the table in her kitchen eating her food. And suddenly she was ravenous. Before Owen could say anything she went to the refrigerator and dug through for anything she could shove in her mouth. Three cheese sticks, great. Good enough. It would barely take the edge off, but at least it was something.

"Make her some food, kid," Andre told Vega.

The young werewolf jumped to his feet without any backtalk and started digging through her cupboards with an almost unnerving familiarity.

Stasia put the cheese stick wrappers down and looked at the other two men. "Anyone want to tell me what's going on? Besides me turning into a werewolf."

Before either could answer, she heard a pained groan from the other room.

She turned her head and looked through the door and caught sight of a bound form sitting against the wall. He wasn't alone.

"Somebody better start talking."

"We were attacked last night," said Owen. "Six men came for you. Armed with stun guns. Gibson sent Vega and Andre to cover us and we fought them off. They're tied up in there. I thought you would want to decide what to do with them."

Six men. Her father had said she was supposed to be safe. Her brother had said she was supposed to be safe. She was supposed to be safe. So how did six men break into her house, cause tons of damage, and nearly kill her, all without the protection her father and brother were supposed to be providing?

Had AR lied to her? Had he used her as bait? Or had he merely been wrong?

It was only a little after five in the morning and it was too early to be caught up with these questions, but she couldn't ignore them.

Owen put his arm around her shoulders and she leaned into his strength. A moment later Vega set a large plate of eggs in front of her.

Her stomach growled again, and before she could make a decision she needed to eat.

She ate. It didn't take long. And then Vega sat more food down in front of her and she ate some more.

She pushed the second plate of eggs away once she was done. "Is this what my new appetite is going to be like?" She liked food, but a normal amount. Not half a dozen eggs in one sitting. Was it only half? She had a feeling Vega had made even more.

"Your body burned a lot of calories last night,"

and Andre. "When we changed we all ate like pigs for about a week, but it eventually normalized. You'll need to eat a lot. Three to five thousand calories a day or thereabouts. But not so much that it will seem outlandish. We're not talking an Olympic athlete's intake."

That was probably twice what she normally ate now, but Stasia would deal with that when the time came. Vega set more food down in front of her and she ate again.

But finally once the dozen eggs were digested along with a couple pieces of toast and, thankfully, about a gallon of coffee, she could start to think about the men who had attacked her and what needed to be done.

"My brother," she decided. The police were useless. And they would ask questions that Stasia didn't want to answer. Besides, if these men had been hired by someone with power, they would be back on the street in no time. AR would make sure the men had to pay for what they did.

It felt more vindictive than she normally was and she wondered if that was part of being a werewolf, but maybe it was just part of being a Selby.

"Are you sure?" Owen asked. "Are you sure you can trust your family?"

"I trust them enough," she said. It was way too

complicated of a relationship to leave to simple trust. Would AR sell her out for the right opportunity? Probably. Would he screw her over if he needed to? Absolutely. Would he do something that would get her killed? Probably not. And would he make someone pay if they hurt her? Yes.

"Can you give us a minute?" Owen asked the other guys, and both of them left.

He waited several seconds, probably waiting until they were far enough away to not overhear what he was about to say.

"What is it?" Stasia asked. Owen looked troubled and she didn't like that look on his face.

"There's something I haven't told you. I haven't told anyone." He was barely talking above a whisper and he kept looking out the entrance to the kitchen as if he expected Vega or Andre to walk in at any moment.

"I thought we said no more secrets." Stasia would have been angry, but he was telling her now and apparently this was a big one.

"It's not like that," he promised. "Or maybe it is. I just needed time to think about it. One of the guys who was working on your security team, I think he was there the night that the ritual was performed on all of us. I'm not absolutely certain, but the faces of those men are burned into my memory. Could be a coincidence. It could have just been a simple job and your family doesn't know. But before you turn anyone over to them I want you to understand that."

So her father might've hired a man who was engaging in occult rituals and the kidnapping of military officials from the US military base in Germany. It sounded possible. But did that mean her father had something to do with it?

"My family is very…" She didn't know how to explain it. "My dad doesn't believe in magic. Neither does my brother. I'm not saying this guy wasn't there. But I have trouble believing that they have something to do with what happened to you and your people. But we definitely need to tell Gibson."

Owen nodded in agreement. "And the guys out there?"

"We're still turning them over to my father. He'll take care of them."

"You know what take care of them means, don't you?"

There was a vicious part in her that wanted to smile, but Stasia held back. She'd made her decision, there was no need to gloat. "I absolutely do. Maybe they should have thought twice before attacking me."

CHAPTER THIRTY-THREE

Gibson wasn't in the city. Owen was kind of glad for that. It meant he could take Stasia out to the farm and show her where they would run as wolves whenever they wanted.

It had taken a little while to get a team of Stasia's father's men to come out and pick up the would be kidnappers, but once they were gone, he and Stasia took off for Pennsylvania.

Stasia seemed full of nervous energy and Owen tried to remember back to the day after his first shift. The whole world seemed new and different, full of opportunities he had never expected.

He reached over and laced their hands together and gave her hand a squeeze. He didn't have reassuring words to give her. He couldn't say that everything would be all right as long as they were together, even if he sort of believed it. The world was changing around them. They were changing. But maybe that was okay.

"Do you think he's going to be angry?" Stasia asked, hitting on a thought that Owen had been avoiding for a while.

"He's not the type to get angry. He gets disappointed." Gibson wasn't quite as good at acting disappointed as Owen's mother was, but the man was pretty damn good. And thinking of his mother, Owen wondered if he should be getting ready to introduce Stasia to her. He kept that thought to himself. They would deal with that later.

They ended up at the farm after about a two hour drive. Gibson's car was parked in the garage. No one else was there, and Owen was glad for that.

He didn't want to see the angry looks on his packmates' faces when they found out he had kept this information from them. But had he really? What could he have said? He knew what some of their abductors looked like? It was just as possible that everyone else knew the same thing. Now he just had more information.

"I'll back you up if you want to run away," Stasia offered with a gentle smile.

"I love you." The words tipped out without a thought, but they were real, true. She was here with him even after going through one of the most traumatic experiences a person could go through. One they had absolutely no preparation for. And yet she was comforting him.

Stasia smiled and raised their clasped hands to kiss the back of his hand. "Let's go do this."

It was okay that she didn't say it back. It was still new. Way too new. People had called Owen impulsive before, but this was impulsive even for him. He didn't care. He knew that Stasia was the one for him and there was no reason to ignore that.

Besides, she had already called herself his mate. That had to mean something.

They headed inside the cabin and Owen found Gibson in his office. He wasn't surprised to see Owen and Stasia; he had known they were coming.

"You look well," he told Stasia, looking her up and down as if checking to see if any of her werewolf traits were peeking out through her human skin. Gibson knew how it worked, at least as well as the rest of them knew, but Stasia was the first new addition to their pack, the first one added through a bite and not through a ritual. They would have to see if that changed things.

"I am well," Stasia agreed. "Not well rested, but not likely to lose control of my wolf and terrorize the city."

Gibson laughed. "If you want to run, you're welcome. We have plenty of land here and the neighbors are not nosy."

It was very true, and Owen looked forward to the day when he could go on a run in his other skin with Stasia at his side. Would she want to go today? He supposed it all depended on how well Gibson reacted to what he was about to say.

"We didn't come here because of Stasia's shift," said Owen as he took a seat. Stasia sat down in the chair next to him.

"Really?" asked Gibson. "Then why are you here?"

There was no sense wasting time. "It's about what happened in Germany."

Gibson looked confused. "I know what happened in Germany. I was there. Unless you've been holding out on me."

Owen winced. He *had* been holding out. "I remember the faces of some of the men who kidnapped us. Or at least the ones who held us before the ritual started. And a few days ago, I'm almost certain I saw one of them working on the security detail that Stasia's brother hired. His name is Russ Hill and I saw personnel files for all of the security team, but there was no mention of a trip to Germany. He was supposed to just be regular security. But I think he was there." The more Owen spoke, the more sure he became.

Russ Hill had been there that night in the Black Forest. He'd been holding a gun and standing on the periphery, determined to keep Owen and his pack members in the magic circle. He didn't know how Hill had come to be there or if he knew about werewolves and magic, but it was the first real lead they had on the people who had hurt them.

Gibson didn't look shocked. He didn't even look surprised. "Russ Hill," he said, like he was testing out the syllables. "Can't say I've heard of him. Do you still have the personnel file?"

Owen pulled out his phone and brought up the information before sharing it to Gibson's email. Gibson opened it on his computer and took a look. There was a personnel picture of Hill that had been taken by the Selby Group as well as a picture that might have been from social media. He didn't smile and he wore a generic looking suit. He could have been anyone. Just looking at the picture Owen would not have recognized him. But when he saw him in person, he knew.

"This is the guy?" asked Gibson.

"He doesn't look like much, but he was there." The sense of torch fire tickled Owen's nose as a flashback threatened to pull him in. Stasia reached out and grabbed his hand, anchoring him in the present.

"You're not the only one who recognized someone that night," Gibson admitted. "And I still have some friends back in Germany who might be able to look into some things. I think we've waited to figure out what happened to us for long enough. We're healthy now, and our pack is growing. We need to know who we are, what we are. We can't just sit around and live with this any longer. This is going to change things. We might be kicking a hornets' nest, are you ready?" Gibson didn't look at Owen when he asked—the question was for Stasia. She was the newest member of their pack, and her life was the one being disrupted the most at this moment.

But Stasia smiled. "I guess that will make my life as your doctor more interesting."

CHAPTER THIRTY-FOUR

THE NEWS that Owen gave to Gibson didn't send the world into a frenzy. As a matter of fact, things started to calm down in the two weeks after that. There were no more attempts to kidnap Stasia and she and Owen settled in to something new and comfortable.

And wonderful.

His things had started migrating to her house. Slowly at first, and then she suddenly noticed that he had taken over half of her closet. Eventually Stasia asked him when she could expect a rent check, but Owen just laughed and offered to pay in sexual favors.

It was easy, and fun, and freeing.

She was growing into her life as a werewolf and already had plans to start researching the limits of what that meant with her pack. She was their doctor now and while they weren't getting into scrapes that needed medical attention every week, she had more skills than just sewing up wounds.

She and Em were able to squeeze in a final dinner before her sister left for her tour, and Em had only spent about half that night pestering her with questions about lycanthropy. The other half of the night had been spent complaining about issues with her own security detail and Stasia had half an idea that Em was going to end up asking one of the pack to come help her out before the tour was done.

And it was finally little Emmy's birthday party. Stasia had made as many excuses as she could, but her family was persistent and it was the perfect opportunity to show her mate off to everyone.

She just hoped that AR didn't rub it in her face that he was technically the reason she and Owen had met. That would be completely insufferable.

"You're sure they're not going to be weird?" Owen asked as he pulled his car into the private parking lot of her father's building.

Stasia grimaced. "Yes, they're going to be weird. They're always weird. But you're a werewolf. You can handle weird." She leaned in close and gave him a kiss on the cheek. "And if you behave, I'll make it worth your while."

"Really? How?" His eyes shifted to that wolfish

yellow that she was growing familiar with before quickly shifting back to their human brown. Owen was working hard to get control of his wolf, and he was getting better at it. He said that now that his wolf had claimed his mate he was happy to cooperate and let the human make most of the decisions.

"I was thinking we could go for a run later."

"It's like you read my mind." Stasia wasn't talking about the human kind of run. No, this would be the kind of run that took place on four legs. But they had to get through the family gauntlet first.

They ran into thirteen-year-old Heidi and fifteen-year-old Ally first, the two girls playing some kind of game near the entrance to the penthouse. Tabitha, the sister closest in age to her, was in the kitchen drinking wine with AR and Ethan, her twenty-two-year-old brother. Thomas wasn't there, since he was in college in Europe and apparently that was a good enough excuse to get out of the party. Neither was Selby, the one other sibling that was older than Stasia. But Selby didn't come to family events, being her father's not-so-secret love child.

She could see Owen mouthing names as he met everyone, and she had a feeling that he had been studying.

Riley and her daughter Emmy were sitting with

Stasia's father in the living room, surrounded by what had to be hundreds of gifts. The four-year-old looked ready to start crying. Riley had a faraway look in her eyes that made her look older than her twenty-three years, and Armand Selby was the picture of a doting father.

Stasia had seen that look before in her other stepmother's eyes. Divorce was around the corner. She only hoped that Riley could afford a good lawyer.

Stasia gripped Owen's hand tight and introduced him to her father and Riley, and she was in a good enough mood that she even gave baby Emmy a hug.

There was plenty to drink and enough food to feed an army. The whole party was miserable, though it got better when a few kids from Emmy's preschool showed up with their mothers in tow.

"Who's this?" Tabitha asked her when Stasia and Owen made it back to the kitchen to hide out by the food and drinks.

She didn't like the tone of her sister's voice. She and Tabitha had never really gotten along. Her father had dumped Stasia's mom for Tabitha's mom and Stasia hadn't yet known that that was just what Armand Selby did. But by the time she figured that out, the resentment was already in place and she and Tabitha had never been close.

"Mob muscle, what do you think?" Anyone else, and Stasia probably would have had a normal conversation. Or as normal as any conversation went with any of her siblings who weren't her.

"You're not still having trouble, are you?" AR came up beside them and shook Owen's hand. "I thought the contract was over. "

"We're dating now," Stasia told her siblings.

"And you brought him here? It must be serious." That was from Tabitha.

"That it is. And I think this counts as doing our duty. Owen and I are going to cut out."

"Dad won't like that," Tabitha warned. Beside her AR was nodding in agreement.

"Dad doesn't like anything. And he's not even going to notice." She'd said hi, she'd done her duty. There was nothing else to worry about.

Tabitha shrugged. "See you at the wedding."

"What wedding?" Had Stasia missed something?

That actually made Tabitha laugh. "Yours. Obviously."

Stasia's eyes got wide and she didn't know how to react to that.

Werewolf, she could handle.

Mate, she could handle.

Bride? That was a bit of a stretch.

Owen put a hand on her back and led her out of

the penthouse. They made it all the way to the elevator before he burst out laughing.

"What?"

"That wasn't nearly as bad as I thought it would be." He gasped it out between bouts of laughter.

"It was worse, right?" It had to be worse. Stasia felt like she needed to shower just to get the awkwardness off of her.

"We survived."

The elevator counted down the floors as they headed to the parking garage, and just as they were about to get to the last floor, Stasia wrapped an arm around Owen and leaned into him. "I love you."

Owen smiled and kissed her.

CHAPTER THIRTY-FIVE

THEY RAN as wolves for hours. It wasn't Stasia's first run, but every single time her paws padded across the soft forest floor it felt new. Scents swirled around her and the night was alive with possibility.

Owen ran, she chased. And then when she overtook him he was the one chasing, barking and pouncing at her, determined to win in a game with no rules and no losers. But eventually the run had to come to an end. There was a sweet temptation that called to her to stay on four legs and forget about her old life.

But that temptation was weak compared to the thought of waking up next to Owen in human skin.

They made it back to the cabin and went through the process of shifting and washing and eating. Wolfishness burned a lot of calories, and Stasia was eating more than she'd ever eaten in her life. Yet she still felt like she could eat more.

Werewolf life had its perks.

She'd had big plans for her mate following their appearance at Emmy's birthday party, but with the run over and her stomach full, all she wanted to do was curl up and sleep for a week. And judging by the way Owen's eyes were drooping, he felt the same.

They ended up snuggled together in one of the beds in the room they were using. It was a tight fit, but Stasia wasn't sleeping apart from her man if she didn't have to.

"I had fun," she murmured as she teetered between wakefulness and sleep.

"It wasn't so bad," Owen agreed.

"Wait. What? What wasn't so bad?" She could still smell hints of the green night air and her body hummed with sated excitement from running as a wolf. There was *nothing* bad about it.

"The party." Owen turned a bit, pulling her closer. "Your family was nice."

"Nice?" Clearly he was delusional. "They were polite, I guess. I still don't see why we needed to be there." Did that make her a bad sister? Maybe. But she was pretty sure little Emmy had no idea who she was.

"They're family." Owen said it like that explained everything. "Can't wait for you to meet mine."

"What? When?" Yeah, that was a thing couples did. Stasia knew that. But it wasn't something Owen could just *spring* on her like that. "When, Owen?" she asked again when he didn't answer. But he had slipped into sleep and none of her prodding could wake him.

Luckily Stasia's own exhaustion was too strong for her momentary panic to override it, and she soon followed her mate into sleep.

Kisses trailing down her stomach woke her up and Stasia stretched into Owen's caress. Her made knew *exactly* how to wake her up and she loved it. She'd never been more sated, more in tune with another person. She didn't know how she'd been blessed with Owen, but she wasn't going to take him for granted.

Not ever.

She arched up as his tongue found her core and delved in, waking her to pleasure and letting her neurons explode with it. She moaned and said words she'd probably want to take back at some point, filthy promises she'd never be able to repay.

Or maybe she would. With Owen, the possibilities were endless.

She let out a curse as her mate did something

particularly wicked that had her eyes rolling back in her head. "God, yes." She needed him to never stop, not ever.

The sensations overran her and Stasia surrendered to them. At some other time she might have felt self-conscious from feeling this much, but Owen brought her the freedom to experience everything with no shame.

He knew what she wanted and he wanted to give it to her. He *wanted* her writhing above him or beneath him or beside him. Any configuration so long as it was the two of them. He was her partner in every way, her mate.

Did she believe in fate?

Stasia couldn't focus on believing in anything besides Owen's tongue at the moment, but from the intensity of what she was feeling it was impossible to believe this was anything but pre-ordained. It couldn't be possible to feel this much, to love this much, to need this much without some cosmic power pulling the strings somewhere.

Or maybe that was just fanciful dreaming. As another wave of pleasure rolled over her, Stasia couldn't make herself latch onto any one thought.

And then Owen pulled away from her and she wanted to cry out in protest. What did he think he was doing? She needed him.

"Now." That was about all she could manage to say.

But Owen knew what she meant and he guided himself to her entrance, teasing his way in and filling her up just like he was born to do.

She reached out and grabbed his hand, linking their fingers together as he plunged inside of her, their bodies moving together as one.

Owen's eyes slipped to that wolfish yellow, and though Stasia couldn't feel anything, she was sure her own eyes matched his. Her teeth ached and her wolf was rising to the surface, not enough to shift, not without her control, but making her more.

Owen bared his neck and Stasia reared up, biting him just as he'd marked her, claiming him as her mate in the way of wolves.

It was the most natural thing in the world to keep him like this, to come together.

Something settled deep within her, an awareness of Owen that went beyond the spiritual. Mate. Lover. Protector. He was all of those things to her and more.

Forever.

She came with a gasp as Owen emptied into her, the certainty of their connection snapping into place. She had no time to catch her breath as he captured her mouth with hers in a searing kiss.

It was overwhelming and perfect and she wanted

to capture this moment forever.

They settled down after a few more fevered kisses, but they couldn't stop touching.

"What do you think we should do tomorrow?" Owen asked as he stroked circles on her tender skin.

Stasia smiled. "More of this. Just the two of us."

Owen chuckled. "Someone's bound to look for us eventually."

"As long as we're together, I'm happy." And she was. For maybe the first time in her life she was really, truly happy, and as long as she had Owen that wasn't about to change.

Thank you for reading Hunting Season!

I'd appreciate it so much if you would consider leaving a review.
The Guarded by the Shifter series will continue with *On the Prowl*.

WANT A FREE BOOK?

Sign up at the link below to receive a free book straight to your inbox!
Link: https://signup.katerudolph.net/subscribe

Explore more shifter romance with The Alpha Heist.

The alpha keeps what's his...

No one steals from Luke Torres. His fortress is legend and his pack of lions are deadly, ready to face any threat. When Luke meets Mel, she knocks his socks off with a scorching kiss, but when they meet again, they are captor and captive in a deadly gave of cat vs. cat.

The thief is up to the task...

From the moment Mel takes the assignment, she knows that it should be impossible. But for the supernatural world's foremost thief, impossible is an irresistible challenge. Especially when the payment for this job will get her one step closer to revenge. When the jobs goes belly up, she finds herself in the lion's den and facing off with the most alluring man she's ever met.

One alpha, one thief, and an adventure of a lifetime.

The thief takes what she wants, but the alpha keeps what's his...

Join shifter thief Mel as she clashes with lion alpha Luke in an explosive trilogy of two opposites who can't keep away from one another.

Also available in audio!

The Alpha Heist

Entangled with the Thief

In the Alpha's Bed

Zulir Warrior Mates

Kidnapped humans. Alien Warriors. Electric wings.

The Zulir Warrior Mates series brings you human heroines and heroes abducted from Earth who find love – and wings! – with the alien warriors who rescue them.

Also available in audio!

Synnr's Saint

Synnr's Hope

Synnr's Spark

Mated to the Alien

Fated Mate Alien Romance

Detyens are doomed to die young if they don't find their fated mates.

Follow along as these mated pairs fight off aliens, corrupt dictators, prejudiced humans, pirates, and more! The books can be read or listened to in any order, though some characters show up in multiple stories.

Select books available in audio.

Pick a book and jump into the action today!

Ruwen

Tyral

Stoan

Cyborg

Krayter

Kayleb

Shayn

Braxtyn

Doryan

Dekon

Detyen Warriors

Detya was destroyed a hundred years ago. These

doomed warriors are out to find justice… and their mates.

The Detyen Warriors series brings you kick butt heroines, alpha alien heroes, fated mates, and relationships strong enough to span the galaxy!

The entire series is also available in audio!

Soulless

Ruthless

Heartless

Faultless

Endless

Alien Holiday Romance

Christmas… in space????

These alien holiday romances look beyond Earth's winter holidays and ring in the season across the galaxy!

Select titles available in audio.

Snowed in with the Alien Beast

The Alien's Winter Gift

The Alien Reindeer's Wild Ride

Trapped with her Alien Mate

Alien Outlaws

Outlaws, schemes, and love… it's all there in the Alien Outlaws series…

Andie Munster is sick of life on Ixilta, the planet she got dumped on after being abducted from Earth six years ago. And when the mysterious and dangerous Xandr shows up looking for a way off the planet, she's half-prisoner, half-co-conspirator in a wild rush to escape.

Rogue Alien's Escape

Rogue Alien's Woman

Rogue Alien's Secret

Rogue Alien's Legacy

Save with box sets!

Aliens. Shifters. Warriors. Mates. Get them all wrapped together in these special box sets. Save up to 30% off the price of buying the individual books, depending on the series!

Alien Outlaws: The Complete Series

Mated to the Alien Volume One (also available in audio)

Mated to the Alien Volume Two

Mated to the Alien Volume Three

Mated to the Alien Volume Four

Stealing the Alpha: The Complete Series (also available in audio)

The Mate Bundle

Detyen Warriors Volume One (also available in audio)

Detyen Warriors Volume Two (also available in audio)

Standalone Paranormal and Sci-Fi Romance:

Crashed

Mated on the Moon

Mated to the Alien Dragon

Marked

Bear in Mind

Alpha's Mercy

Gemma's Mate

Howling for You

Find more by Kate Rudolph at www.katerudolph.net

ABOUT KATE RUDOLPH

Kate Rudolph is paranormal and sci-fi romance writer who lives in Indiana. She loves writing about kick butt heroines and the steamy heroes who love them. She's been devouring romance novels since she was too young to be reading them and had to hide her books so no one would take them away. She couldn't imagine a better job in this world than writing romances and sharing them with her fellow readers.

If you enjoyed this story, please consider leaving a review.

www.ingramcontent.com/pod-product-compliance
Lightning Source LLC
Chambersburg PA
CBHW061622190726
48288CB00007B/2426

9 781953 748072